"I'm not here to sell books," Margaret said, "but to ask a question. Have you ever heard of a young artist called Benedict Howe?"

The twinkle in Mr. Bottom's eyes vanished and he drew his bushy eyebrows together in a frown.

"I've heard the name, as it happens," he said slowly. . . .

"What would Benedict Howe want with blank sheets of paper from a very old estate book . . . ?"

"I immediately suspect that Benedict Howe needed old paper because he intends to forge Old Master drawings and pass them off as the real thing for a lot of money. He'd need paper of the right age to do that."

"But surely he couldn't get away with it," Margaret said.

"My dear lady Margaret, he could—and he has. I speak from personal experience."

By Joyce Christmas
Published by Fawcett Books:

Lady Margaret Priam mysteries:
SUDDENLY IN HER SORBET
SIMPLY TO DIE FOR
A FÊTE WORSE THAN DEATH
A STUNNING WAY TO DIE
FRIEND OR FAUX
IT'S HER FUNERAL
A PERFECT DAY FOR DYING
MOURNING GLORIA
GOING OUT IN STYLE
DYING WELL

Betty Trenka mysteries:
THIS BUSINESS IS MURDER
DEATH AT FACE VALUE
DOWNSIZED TO DEATH
MOOD TO MURDER

Lady Margaret Priam/Betty Trenka mysteries:
A BETTER CLASS OF MURDER
FORGED IN BLOOD

FORGED IN BLOOD

A Lady Margaret Priam/
Betty Trenka Mystery

Joyce Christmas

FAWCETT BOOKS • NEW YORK

A Fawcett Book
Published by The Ballantine Publishing Group
Copyright © 2002 by Joyce Christmas

www.ballantinebooks.com

ISBN 0-449-00714-6

Manufactured in the United States of America

First Edition: August 2002

10   9   8   7   6   5   4   3   2   1

For
Frank Santos, super friend,
and
Cecilia Wessinger, super woman

PROLOGUE

"*I*'M NOT going," Betty Trenka said firmly. "I'll call Lady Margaret and cancel. This time I mean it."

Ted Kelso, Betty's friend and neighbor on Timberhill Road in East Moulton, Connecticut, said with equal firmness, "You'll go. You've hinted at your doubts for the past few weeks, but you won't disappoint me, or Lady Margaret, or Sid Edwards. Or yourself."

"I'm an old lady. My arthritis . . ." Betty began. Ted moved his wheelchair across the living area so that he could look her in the eye. She knew he saw her as standing in for him, being a substitute Ted, seeing the things he wanted to see again. She was able, as he was not, to walk through the Roman Forum, gaze at the Colosseum, sip an espresso at a sidewalk cafe.

"Elizabeth, don't try that excuse on me, of all people." Ted sounded angry. "Your arthritis is in your imagination or the imagination of that quack who manages your health. You'll get around just fine, and besides, Lady Margaret will see to it that you go first class all the way. Everything will be handled for you—five-star hotels, people to fetch and carry, the best of everything."

"I don't know how to behave with all those fancy people. I'm just a retired office manager, not a woman of the world."

"You managed to get along in New York society without trouble. . . ."

"By virtue of people believing I was somebody I wasn't," Betty said grimly. "I hated that. And I'm so ignorant. I won't appreciate what I'm seeing. And if I pretend I do, I'll be shown up as a pure fraud. I just can't go. I don't have time to get ready."

She had less than four weeks to prepare for the flight across the Atlantic with her new friend Lady Margaret Priam. They would fly to London, then travel to the countryside to Priam's Priory, Lady Margaret's ancestral home, for the wedding of Margaret's brother, the Earl of Brayfield. Next they would return to London and then travel on to Rome to visit Prince Aldo Castrocani, the father of Margaret's young friend Prince Paul, at his villa near Rome. They'd see St. Peter's, the Forum, the Colosseum, and no doubt many dusty villas and formal gardens much like those in her guidebooks about Italy, if not the very same places.

Gardens and gardening were not her passion. Indeed, her ability to keep a row of marigolds thriving for a summer was still in doubt. Last year's attempt had been a failure. The lavish interiors of palazzi and English country houses also didn't move her— domestic matters were simply of no interest. In any case, her tastes were simpler than gilded mirrors and damask upholstery. Even her determined mother had failed to educate her in the domestic arts. The stocky, first-generation Czech housewife had never turned Betty into a fine homemaker, suitable for marriage. So Betty had lived through her childhood and teens in the small upstate Connecticut industrial town without making a single successful poppy-seed roll or *halupke*.

When she'd escaped to work near Hartford for Sid Edwards, she'd cooked only enough to keep herself from starving in the simple, neat apartments she'd inhabited. She hadn't gone hungry for the more than forty years she'd lived on her own, but she'd never developed a passion for preparing gourmet meals or even the sturdy peasant dishes of her ancestors. At best, she'd venture back home and allow her mother to feed her the traditional food, all the while shaking her head sadly at her daughter's barren life.

Back then, the distance between Betty's hometown and the city seemed enormous, and she'd conquered that. Now she faced an even longer journey into the unknown. Even worse than the unknown was her awareness of her lack of sophistication and her ignorance of art, history, or even the proper way to behave in the company of English aristocrats and Italian nobility.

Her father had been opposed to educating women. Why would they need to recognize a Botticelli or understand a poem when their preordained role was to care for a husband's needs, to bear and raise children, and to attend Mass on Sundays? So

Betty had independently attended a secretarial school, despite his objections, and still read whatever books she fancied. When a husband and children were not forthcoming, she'd built a different sort of life, and she'd been happy with it, even if Pop wasn't. There had been one great love, but eventually everything had come crashing down.

Now, far from the work she'd loved and the office that had been her home and haven for decades, she was again creating a new life. She could do it, thanks to the money provided by Sid Edwards when they'd both been forced to retire after Sid Junior took over Edwards & Son.

"Taking tea on the lawn of Priam's Priory is silly and pretentious," Betty said. "It's a waste of money to send me to Rome to look at paintings of Madonnas and martyred saints."

One Madonna looked pretty much like another to her: a sweet face, elegant drapery, and a plump Christ Child looking far wiser than any of the few naked real-life infants she'd ever reluctantly encountered.

When she was a child, she'd dutifully listened to the nuns recount the lives of the saints and had been thrilled by the tales of martyrdom, but since she had fallen away from the Church of her youth, the graphic details of religious paintings no longer interested her, and the significance of saintly sacrifice had no meaning.

"You'll go," Ted said.

"Ted, I'm a senior citizen, well into my sixties,

and quite old enough to decide what I do or don't want to do. I'll spend an easy summer tending those damned marigolds in my backyard, keeping Tina's food dish filled, and visiting Sid at the nursing home. He's making good progress recovering from the stroke. He'll understand my cold feet."

But would he? He'd always wanted her to travel abroad. They'd talked about the trips she would take. Would Tina, the miserable black cat she'd inherited, understand why the food dish was being filled by the Saks boys from next door instead of by Betty? No, Tina cared only that the tuna was there on schedule.

"Yes, you'll go," Ted said once more. "You'll do what I can't." He looked so wistful there in his wheelchair that she began to feel guilty about backing out of the trip. "And don't tell me you can't handle any situation that pops up. You're a pleasant conversationalist and you can hold your own, whether it's the Queen or a dairymaid. You have your tickets and your passport. You're ready to go. You even said you were listening to conversational Italian tapes."

"*Si,*" Betty said awkwardly, "but I'm not very good at Italian yet."

"That's no problem. Italians are delighted to have you converse in pantomime. You act out the verbs, point to objects, and they like to guess what you mean. You simply *must* go. At least for my sake."

"You're right, of course. It would be cowardly to back out now."

Ted grinned. "Whatever you are, Elizabeth, you are not a coward."

"I can't wait to go," Lady Margaret Priam told Prince Paul Castrocani when she called him.

Margaret loved going back to Priam's Priory. For nearly a decade she'd been in her element as a decorative, sought-after denizen of New York society, but she'd only been home once or twice. And after some years of close friendship with Prince Paul, the son of hugely rich Carolyn Sue Hoopes, the former Princess Castrocani, she was curious to meet his father.

"I wanted to be sure that it had been arranged for Miss Trenka and me to visit your father."

"*Certo*. He is even now commanding the servants to repair the plaster and the fountains and paint the balconies so that you will return to America with tales of how prosperous the villa looks and you will then repeat them to my mother, who will ache with regret that she ever left him and took her millions of dollars back to Dallas."

"It seems quite a bother to try to impress me," Margaret said.

Paul chuckled. "My father is as concerned about presenting *la bella figura* as any other Italian. I am sure he is now visiting his tailor for a new suit in the latest fashion, and his barber to perhaps darken the silvered hairs on his head. He is delighted at the prospect of your visit, and at the possibility of causing my mother intense longing for their distant and happy times together. I have tried to convince him that Carolyn Sue regrets nothing and certainly longs for nothing. She can purchase anything she desires, even, indeed, happiness if it wears a Neiman Marcus or Tiffany label."

"I shall miss you both," Margaret said, and there was a longish pause.

"De Vere is not in just now," Paul said finally. "Is that why you called me?"

"Of course not." But it was, in part. Sam De Vere had been Margaret's faithful beau for several years, during which time he had worked as a New York City police detective. Now he had decided to retire early from police work and become a gentleman farmer in New Jersey, a place where Margaret was reluctant to settle, so she had seen little of him recently. She was fairly certain that another marriage was not her fate, not after the unsuccessful first one. De Vere and Paul shared a spacious apartment in Chelsea in a building owned by Paul's mother, so the rent was suitably low and the surroundings comfortable and convenient for both of them.

"I'll ring you again before I leave," Margaret said. "I have so much thinking to do to be sure everything is perfect for the wedding."

"And I will remind De Vere to call you."

"Really, that's not why I rang you. Although it would be good to see him, or at least speak to him, before I leave."

"He's not in the city. He may have gone to Connecticut for fishing, or out to New Jersey to look at some property with that real estate man. . . ."

"Not Richard Centner."

"That's the one. He was mixed up with that woman who threw the birthday party for her husband."

"I wouldn't trust him to sell me . . . well, never mind. If it makes Sam happy to look at grassy acres and quaint little bungalows, I shan't complain."

Later that day, Betty did call Margaret, but merely to consult her about what to wear to the wedding.

In her six decades and more of life, Elizabeth Trenka had never been overly concerned about clothes. Neat, clean, and businesslike for the office, neat and casual for home, with emphasis on denim skirts and jeans, heavy sweaters, and comfortable shoes. Lately, however, it seemed that she was finding herself entrapped in situations where clothes made a difference, at least to others. People assumed that because she was at a fashionable society cocktail party, she must be a member of fashionable society. True, an elegant outfit plus the very good jewelry Sid had given her over the years seemed to transform her, in the eyes of others, into someone they believed was minor European nobility. Once when that had happened, she'd been terribly embarrassed, but she'd had the wit to carry it off without lying or being exposed as a fraud. She laughed about it later, but at the time . . .

"Some sort of summery frock will do nicely," Margaret said, "and no, it needn't be a long dress. Nothing white, of course. Black is also unacceptable, although I've noticed it's a very fashionable color at American weddings. Yes, you'll need a hat, nothing fancy. We're going to have a wonderful time. Now, don't worry about your dress. I'm sure you'll look very nice."

An appropriate dress for the wedding of an earl surely wouldn't be too difficult to find; at least a long dress wasn't expected. But then there was the matter of the proper attire for socializing with an Italian prince, and what she would need to wear as a tourist in Rome. She didn't think she'd have the opportunity to attend an audience with the Pope— although her cousin, Sister Rita, a dedicated nun living in Boston, would be thrilled by the idea—but Betty's wobbly attachment to the Church of her childhood didn't place that possibility very high on her wish list. She'd send Rita a postcard from the Vatican.

"I ought to go home and make a list," she told Ted. "I guess that means I'm really going on this trip."

As she was about to leave, Ted said, "I saw my doctor the other day. . . ." Ted's car was equipped to make driving possible for him. "I didn't want to tell you too much before now, but he's optimistic about my condition."

Ted had never discussed his condition with her in any detail. She knew only that fifteen or twenty years earlier, he had received an untested vaccine that had reacted in a way that slowly robbed him of his mobility.

"What did he say? You have to tell me now."

"He sees real improvement. It may even be reversible. There are new treatments coming. And it may be that by the time you come home, we'll walk about my garden together."

"That would be wonderful, Ted." She felt almost tearful at the news.

"So I want you out of the way while the doc and I explore the possibilities. If nothing works out, I want to think that you are seeing new sights, meeting new people. If I'm left without hope, at least I'll know that you are forging on in my place."

"I'm going," Betty said. "I'll be a perfect stand-in for you. I'll see everything and tell you about every step I take. Now I just have to arrange to get to the airport in New York."

"Good girl, you're a good girl," Ted said. "And I'll even drive you to New Haven, where you can catch a limo to Kennedy Airport. Margaret will be there to meet you at the British Airways counter. It's all settled."

"How did you arrange that?"

"I called her. I knew that you had some doubts about the trip, so I wanted everything to be in place, because in the end, I knew you'd go."

CHAPTER 1

THE FLIGHT from New York's Kennedy Airport to Gatwick Airport in England gave Margaret time to confide to Betty her concerns about her brother's upcoming wedding.

"The only matter that troubles me is my brother's choice of a bride. David is a good catch for any young woman of his class, but he looked elsewhere. He's not rich. The upkeep of large estates like the Priory costs a good deal, and money isn't exactly flooding in from agricultural activities. He's detailed losses due to the outbreak of foot-and-mouth disease. The Priory's dairy herd had to be destroyed; the sheep met a similar end. Fortunately mad cow disease never appeared, so the Priam cows remained sane even as they were sent to their execution."

"How sad," Betty said, wondering only briefly why she had suddenly become Margaret's confidante. Perhaps she imagined that Betty was a mother figure. Well, she'd been mistaken for a countess in the past. Perhaps Margaret had no one else to whom she could express her worries.

"The village of Upper Rime is in bad shape economically, so David insisted that the villagers send no wedding gifts. But apparently gifts have come pouring in, to the delight of his affianced, who loves to open them and carefully record who sent what. Still, he might have chosen someone to wed other than the daughter of the local pub owner.

"He might have found a wealthy wife, even a wealthy American, the way Prince Aldo did, although girls with the financial clout of Carolyn Sue don't often pass through the doors of Priam's Priory. If our mother had lived longer, she would certainly have arranged for David to meet someone more suitable than Alice Grant. They call her Lys. Pleasant as she is, Lys is not someone trained to run the Priory. It's a big Tudor house built on the ruins of an old religious establishment closed down by Henry the Eighth.

"But she does have an Oxford degree, and seems capable of producing a baby viscount to keep the title of Earl of Brayfield alive and in the family. Perhaps that is all that is necessary—an heir. And she'll manage the house to the best of her ability. My mother established a pattern that continues still, years after her death."

"It will turn out all right, I'm sure," Betty said sleepily.

While Betty dozed in her seat, Margaret reviewed the upcoming ceremony. The idea of a wedding at the Priory—at the village church, performed by dotty old Uncle Herbert, now a rather distinguished Anglican bishop—appealed to Margaret's sense of romance and tradition. There would be flowers from the Priory's gardens, and a hundred people up from London as well as from even grander country houses across England. The servants would be there in their best clothes, along with the regular patrons of The Riming Man, the leading—indeed only—pub in the village of Upper Rime.

She tried to imagine Jimmy Grant, Lys's father, in a proper gray morning suit guiding his daughter down the aisle. Stop worrying, she told herself. Jimmy will do right by Lys. After all, he had managed to provide the funds for a university education. Then she tried not to imagine what sort of dresses Lys had chosen for her attendants, but surely modern English girls watched the telly and read fashion magazines, and so had some sense of what was proper.

As for food and drink, David would see that there was plenty of good champagne for the reception. Mrs. Domby, the Priory cook and housekeeper for more than three decades, would outdo herself with canapes, and Margaret hoped that David had insisted that she bring in a caterer for the sit-down dinner for a chosen few, which would be held later, after the photographers had done their job. Undoubtedly a photographer from *The Tatler* would be there, since David was a titled and personable young man with many friends. Chloe Waters of Figge Hall, Warwickshire, David's one-time girlfriend, would not miss the wedding, and she alone would attract the press, as she'd been doing for the past few years.

It was just as well that David had not selected

Chloe as his bride. She was a social climber of the sort Margaret knew well from New York society. Chloe was perfectly well bred; her father had plenty of money—acquired in trade, alas—and he expected to be knighted in the near future. While Chloe was pretty enough, she was bland and brainless, with a knack for scandalous behavior that made snickering headlines in the tabloids. Marrying David would have been a distinct leap upward on the social scale. Even now, she would certainly have wangled an invitation to the wedding, if only because there would surely be other titled marital prospects among the guests. With a sinking feeling, Margaret realized that it was conceivable that a member of the Royal family would be in attendance. Her father and mother had known quite a few of the Royals, as did David. Margaret winced at the thought of managing a pack of *Your Highness*es and *Your Grace*s.

Harbert, the Priory's well-trained butler, was long gone, and she had no knowledge of the man who had taken his place. She hoped he could handle the intricacies of a Royal family appearance. At least disreputable cousin Nigel Priam would not appear, being untimely deceased. But the ugly Americans Phyllis and Lester Flood, who had purchased Rime Manor from David, would be there and would behave inappropriately. She imagined Phyllis attempting to curtsey to, say, one of Princess Margaret's offspring. David was acquainted with Viscount Linley and had even bought a piece of expensive furniture Linley crafted for his own special hideaway, the white room with arches that had been the dining hall for the original Priory inhabitants. One could only hope that Linley's mother, Princess Margaret, had more important duties to tend to. Margaret was only grateful that Princes William and Harry were too young to be friends of her brother's. Even Prince Charles was no more than a passing acquaintance.

Betty appeared to be soundly asleep, so Margaret found the crumpled list she'd made back in New York, listing the items that she wasn't sure Lys would remember. Of course, in her experience, Oxford-educated young women believed they knew everything that needed knowing. Still, it couldn't hurt to remind Lys of matters such as:

Flowers (Priory gardens, and Lady What's-it for the bouquet, the one who does everybody's)
Bridal dress (she must have ordered it by now)
Attendants' dresses
Hair (she must have someone who does her)
Attendants (Need four children besides her girl-friends. Whose?)
Music: service and dancing (discourage latter)
Food instructions for Mrs. Domby
Display of gifts—Great Hall, someone to stand guard
Family tiara—where is it kept? (Upstairs safe?)
Bridesmaids' gifts

The first order of business upon arriving in London was to find a hat for herself. Harrods and Harvey Nichols were both close to the flat where they would spend their first night. Since old Potts was to

drive them to the Priory tomorrow, the day before
the ceremony, she would have a little time to look.
If those two shops didn't have a proper hat, she
wouldn't set foot in London again.

Lost in her thoughts, Margaret, too, began to
doze off to the hum of the jet's engines, then sat up
abruptly. The only thing she hadn't worried about
was the weather. It would be a disaster if it rained
on the wedding party.

Margaret mentioned her weather worries to Betty
as she tried on a pile of hats at Harvey Nichols.
"The clouds I see are ominous," she said. "Ah, this
one's rather nice."

"Very pretty," Betty said. The hat was lace-
trimmed. "I thought women at English weddings
wore great beehives of hats or floppy garden party
things. I remember pictures."

"This one will do," Margaret said. "I hope the
Priory is still well-supplied with umbrellas."

"It won't rain," Betty said. "My arthritis kicks in
when rain is coming. I feel perfectly fine."

"You never know in England," Margaret said.

The next morning, a pink-cheeked old man
whom Margaret introduced to Betty as Potts appeared in a Land Rover and drove them through the
countryside to the impressive pile of stone called
Priam's Priory.

Betty had been granted a bedchamber once slept
in by the first Queen Elizabeth, and the next day,
while Margaret fussed about the arrangements for
the wedding, Betty strolled about the estate, trailed

by a friendly golden retriever. A groom showed her the barn and the horses, including one old fellow that was to draw the carriage that would take the bride to the church.

There was no sign of rain clouds as the wedding day dawned. The servants, commanded by Mrs. Domby, were scurrying about making final preparations. Early-arriving guests had to be soothed with food and drink and shown to rooms where the ladies could primp before making their appearance. Potts supervised the parking of vehicles from grand Bentleys to sporty little cars, and guided the guests who chose to walk down the hill to the Romanesque stone church, now fragrant and colorful with flowers gleaned from the Priory's gardens. The bride and her attendants glided down the aisle, the groom looked poised, and Uncle Herbert, distinguished in his vestments, performed the ceremony almost without a hitch, although he did stumble briefly over "Alice Susanna Annabel, do you take . . ." And then they were released into the sunshine.

"It's a perfect June day, and everyone looks lovely, especially Lys. Very pretty girl, thank goodness," Margaret said to Betty after the ceremony, away from the clot of guests surrounding the newly married Earl and Countess of Brayfield.

"I told you it wouldn't rain," Betty said. "Oh, look. That couple looks very familiar."

"The Kents," Margaret said. "The Duke and Duchess of Kent knew my mother well, and me as a child. I'll introduce you. So nice that they appeared for the ceremony, and they even seem to be staying for a bit for the champagne. The photographers are delighted and Lys turned pink at the excitement of having royals at her wedding, and she curtseyed ever so nicely."

Margaret went on to say that she noticed that David wasn't the least impressed, having known the Kents for ages.

When Margaret introduced Betty to the ducal couple, she seemed flustered but then she chatted up the duke and duchess for quite a time.

"I feared I might faint from the excitement," Betty said. "I actually met a duchess. Wait till I tell Ted."

"You handled yourself very well," Margaret said. "Everything is going well, I think. And isn't it nice that we don't have to worry about a murderer in our midst. I seem to have a gift for attracting dead bodies at lovely affairs like this one."

"As do I," Betty said, and looked around nervously.

"Everyone here looks quite benign. I hope our luck holds through the entire trip."

Betty frowned. "I can't help thinking of those Borgias and the Mafia in Italy."

"Don't worry," Margaret said. "The Mafia certainly doesn't murder harmless tourists, and I believe the Borgias are pretty much extinct."

Betty said, "I don't often have the opportunity to meet a duchess. A lovely woman. And the duke! He had some interesting things to say about the obligations of his position, even the dangers posed by being a public figure, although he did mention that he found the wedding most relaxing. Everyone treats me as though I were important."

"You are important."

During the post-wedding champagne toasts, while the guests mingled and lavished praise on the well-organized ceremony, Margaret joined her brother, who was accepting congratulations with his bride at his side.

"Lys has done a marvelous job of putting together the event. The bridal attendants look lovely," Margaret whispered to David.

Lys, overhearing, said, "I asked them to choose their own dresses, the only stipulation being that the gowns be a pastel shade with a flower print." She was distracted briefly by her junior attendants, two little boys and two little girls in tiny gray morning suits and frilly pink gowns respectively. They had behaved admirably.

One of the girls confessed to Margaret that this was her fifth wedding, so she knew the drill very well indeed. Even Margaret felt comfortable in her finery, a pale turquoise dress from Bendel's and the broad-brimmed white straw hat with a sprinkling of lace that she'd found at Harvey Nichols.

Miss Trenka had come up with a rose-colored chiffon dress and a little pink hat that looked quite charming perched atop her pile of heavy hair. Everyone, in fact, looked very nice, and no one turned up dressed defiantly in white, not even the dangerous Chloe, although a couple of David's other spurned romantic interests made statements by wearing chic black. David did not notice.

But Margaret did notice that a burly young man unknown to her had struck up an earnest conversation with Miss Trenka. Margaret thought Betty looked a bit uncomfortable and wondered if she was in need of rescue.

"David, who is that young man talking to Miss Trenka?" She described him gently lest he be a close friend of David's or a very distinguished gentleman who should not be offended.

"Benedict Howe, a friend of Lys's. She met him up at Oxford, some kind of clever fellow." David looked grim. "Never cared for the chap. He claims to be an artist. Lys insisted on inviting him and one or two other Oxford chums."

Margaret suspected that David was jealous of someone who might have been a beau of Lys's. Still, despite Betty's wary expression, the young man seemed well behaved.

"I wonder what they could be talking about," Margaret said. "Not art, certainly. Whilst British Airways was serving us our fourth round of crumpets, strawberry jam, and clotted cream, Miss Trenka admitted that she's fairly ignorant about art." Margaret couldn't decide if she liked Benedict Howe's looks—the slightly unruly hair, a hint of dark stubble as though he hadn't bothered to shave, the vaguely rumpled jacket and trousers. At least he was wearing decent shoes, and he wasn't paint-spattered. His eyes shifted constantly as though he was sizing up which guests to approach when his conversation with Elizabeth wore thin.

"Himself, most certainly. He has quite an ego."

"A successful artist, then?"

"I think not. Lys has brought him to the Priory once or twice. He wanted to have a look at our pictures." The Priams had collected a number of old or possibly just middle-aged masters over the centuries, some of them interesting but only moderately valuable. There was a good Holbein portrait, a second-rate Rembrandt, some Indian miniatures, and lots of old books, but nothing, Margaret believed, worth making a special effort to view.

"I believe he is more or less a fraud," David went on sullenly. "Talks a mighty tale about his art and his career, but I've never seen his work or heard his name mentioned or read about any of his exhibitions. I can't imagine what he read at Oxford—art history, perhaps, if they teach such a thing—but he claims to have studied at some art school in London and at the feet of another self-styled genius as a private student. And, yes, he spent a year or two painting in Rome. He must be telling your Miss Trenka how to enjoy the city, although I imagine his Roman adventures would not be suitable for an elderly spinster to replicate."

David turned back to Lys. She looked very fetching in her ivory lace bridal gown as she chatted with the four handsome children who had participated in the ceremony. The Priam family tiara on her head sparkled in the June afternoon sunshine. At least, Margaret thought, she's good with children. She'll make a suitable mother of the heir to the title, may he come soon.

She edged through the crowd in the direction of

Miss Trenka. Since David didn't think much of the Benedict man, it couldn't hurt to snatch Betty away from him. The wretched Americans, Phyllis and Lester Flood, who were still renovating the manor house near the Priory, were standing about figuratively flapping their hands because they knew no one except for David, who was busy with Lys and well-wishers, and Margaret, whom they hadn't yet approached. Well, they would of course know Jimmy Grant, Lys's father, but he was a bit too far down the social ladder to interest them. She decided at once to steer Benedict in the Floods' direction.

As she plotted her campaign to detach Betty from the artist, she heard a voice raised in an unseemly manner and noted that Lester Flood was haranguing a modestly dressed older man who looked like an estate worker got up in his Sunday best for the wedding. She recognized Toby Mills, a day laborer who had transferred from the Priory to Rime Manor to assist the Floods in their renovation efforts. He seemed to have angered Lester, but this was hardly the place to have it out with the man.

But the first matter of business was Betty.

"So sorry to interrupt, Elizabeth, but I do want to introduce you to my uncle Herbert, the bishop who performed the ceremony. It's best we catch him before he gets too deeply into Mrs. Domby's food and the champagne. He tends to nod off when he's well fed." Margaret turned her smile on the not-too-successful artist. "Hullo, I'm Lady Margaret Priam, David's sister, and now Lys's sister-in-law."

Benedict had piercing dark eyes beneath heavy

brows. For now he stopped his edgy scanning of the guests and looked directly at her. Perhaps he believed that bold eye contact was sexy and compelling.

"I've heard of you, of course," he said. "The sister who sought greener pastures in America. I'm Benedict Howe, an old friend of Lys's. I understand from Miss Trenka that you two are off soon to Italy to visit Prince Aldo Castrocani."

"Ah, yes."

"Do you know him well? He's charming. I got to know him a bit when I was studying art in Rome."

"Actually, I don't know him at all, but his son, Paul, and his former wife, Carolyn Sue, are close friends."

"I know them as well. Paul was an occasional part of my social circle in Rome in the old days. He had a reputation as a jet set playboy. I met his mother once, around the time she was divorcing Aldo. She's said to be very wealthy. Aldo is certainly not rich. But one gets on with shabby Italian nobility as they often have unexpected hidden assets.

"I did once manage to persuade Paul to invite me to visit his father's villa near Rome when the prince was not in residence. The Castrocanis harbor a couple of Renaissance works that I was eager to see, but Aldo is reluctant to show them to outsiders, and he forbids family members from showing them. He won't even openly acknowledge ownership. They're probably worth a fortune, and if he chooses to sell them, he doesn't want the Italian tax authorities to be aware of the prices they'll fetch." Benedict had a sly, calculating expression that made Margaret uneasy. She resolved to telephone Paul that day and find out about Benedict Howe. She hoped he wouldn't turn out to be the murderer who inevitably showed up when she was enjoying a lovely fete. No, she wouldn't allow past experience to prejudice her against him—not until she heard what Paul had to say.

"Elizabeth, we'd best catch up with Uncle Herbert," Margaret said. "Mr. Howe, may I suggest you chat up that couple right over there. They are Mr. and Mrs. Lester Flood, Americans who are decorating a house near here that they purchased from David. They might be interested in large paintings in colors to match their décor. You do paint, I understand?" He nodded. "They're very, very rich, albeit ignorant about art and most things." She managed a conspiratorial wink, and Benedict beamed. "But Mr. Flood seems to be in a temper at the moment, so tread carefully. It doesn't do to offend a patron of the arts."

"They sound ideally suited to my art, which can be in any color they desire. Mrs. Flood is quite an attractive woman, don't you think?" He grinned. "I find older women more interesting than my flutterbug contemporaries such as Chloe Waters. Women like Mrs. Flood usually need only stroking and flattery rather than expensive tokens of affection, and they are generally in a position to offer the tokens rather than receive them."

Margaret examined the figure of Phyllis Flood, now earnestly chatting with the member of Parliament who represented Upper Rime. He looked slightly dazed.

Phyllis's dress was undoubtedly expensive and her hair was nicely coiffed, but she herself was a bit too buxom and matronly to be truly stylish. Phyllis's appearance shouted money, which might be part of her appeal to Benedict. She also wore a perpetual look of discontent, especially now when she glanced at Lester, who was attempting to entertain a bored-looking young woman who had served as one of Lys's bridal attendants.

"I judge that Mrs. Flood is in dire need of distraction," Benedict said, "and I will oblige her. Mr. Flood strikes me as a cannon ready to fire at any minute. I shall be wary of him. May I mention to them that you suggested I introduce myself?"

"By all means," Margaret said. "I should imagine Lester would fancy a portrait of himself as lord of the manor—if you do portraits."

"One of my specialities," he said. "Also large landscapes with meandering brooks. I'm weak on horses, but very strong on ivy-covered Roman ruins. In fact, I am very good at almost everything. They have but to suggest a style and subject, and I can produce it."

"You are made for one another." Margaret and Betty watched him sidle up to the Floods and start talking immediately. "He seems personable enough. Probably not a murderer."

"What? Oh, you mean the sort of person who appears at every opportunity to entangle us in a mess. I'm sure that he's created his own share of trouble in his time. He was telling me some odd tales of intrigue in Rome. But he was quite charming about it."

Benedict's charm seemed to be working still, for in a very few minutes, he and the Floods were chatting cozily. Phyllis was hanging on his every word, and Lester seemed in better temper. Toby Mills slunk off with a look of relief. Then Margaret saw Phyllis playfully tap Benedict's shoulder, an almost coquettish gesture. Lester frowned, and Benedict gestured widely, as though demonstrating the dimensions of a proposed painting. Phyllis glanced toward Margaret and Betty, her face brightening as she recognized Margaret. She waved with unrestrained enthusiasm. Margaret was sure she'd be enjoying Mrs. Flood's company very shortly. Happily, she and Betty soon would be leaving for London so she had an excuse if Phyllis invited them to the manor for tea.

"After your social success in New York, Elizabeth, Phyllis Flood has probably heard of you. She's a true climber of social ladders, constructing the steps from piles of Lester's money."

"I believe I heard her name mentioned at that reception Mrs. Thompson invited me to, when she thought my father was a deceased archduke from Prague."

"She still thinks so," Margaret said. "Now, what were you and Benedict Howe discussing? I don't mean to pry, but Howe says he knows Paul's father."

"That's what we were talking about," Betty said.

"Our trip to Italy, I mean. Mr. Howe indicated that he was planning on traveling to the continent soon and might well pass through Rome. I told him you had booked us into the Hotel d'Inghilterra. I hope that was all right?"

Margaret shrugged. "Rome is a rather small city. We'd likely bump into him at some point, so it doesn't matter if he should happen to turn up on our doorstep. What did you think of him?"

Betty thought for a moment. "I've met his type before," she said slowly. "Rather like a salesman I once knew with a shoddy line of goods to sell. I think very good artists don't feel the need to boast of their work; they just know it's good and behave accordingly. Someone less talented has to make the product sound better than it is. Benedict was bemoaning the lack of vision on the part of critics and dealers and the general public, or rather their failure to comprehend his vision, his art. I take it he's something of a failure in his chosen field?"

"My brother says he is not widely known." Margaret frowned. David was definitely not a connoisseur of fine art, but possibly a jolt of jealousy because of Benedict's old friendship with Lys had caused him to look into the artist's life and career.

"There you are," Betty said. "A man with a shoddy line of goods, wondering why the public scorns him."

The photographer had herded the wedding party and guests into a group with the modest turrets of Priam's Priory in the background, the duke and duchess prominently displayed on either side of the bridal couple, and Uncle Herbert, still in his vestments, raising his champagne glass in a sort of tipsy toast to the entire group.

"I wonder how many glasses he's had," Margaret said. "Mrs. Domby knows to keep an eye on him, and our old butler did as well, but the new butler, Simmons or something, isn't well versed in Herbert's tendencies."

Then she and Betty saw one of the tiny attendants, a little blond girl of six or seven, grasp Uncle Herbert's free hand and lead him away to a chair under a large leafy tree.

"A little child shall lead them," Margaret said under her breath. "Now what?"

Lys appeared to be trying to pull Benedict Howe to the forefront of the group, and he was resisting quite firmly. And just as the photographer raised his camera for a shot, Benedict ducked his head so all that could be seen was the thatch of hair on his crown.

"Mr. Howe does not care to be photographed," Betty said. "I wonder why if he is so eager for fame."

The incident quickly passed, and the photographer concentrated on the duke and duchess, the Earl of Brayfield and his new countess, and of course, the adorable children. Then Margaret was summoned to pose with her brother and sister-in-law.

Margaret is a lovely woman, Betty thought to herself. *I hope she will see that I get some of the pictures. Ted will want to see them.* She had been lax about sending him the promised postcards, but these few days in England had been a dizzying whirl of activity.

Benedict had escaped from the group and was making his way toward Betty. "I think I had best be heading back to London, Miss Trenka," he said. "I look forward to seeing you in Rome. I know all the best sidewalk cafes and restaurants. Before I leave, I'm just going to nip into the Priory for a moment to have a look at the portraits in the Great Hall and the library. One is a very fine painting by Holbein the Younger that's seldom reproduced. The old earl apparently didn't care to have the unwashed masses admiring his belongings, but David and Lys won't mind. Please tell the countess that I had to leave, but will ring her before I set off for Rome." He paused. "No, you don't have to make a special point of giving a message—just if she happens to ask about me. See you and Margaret soon then, I hope." He strode away toward the big house and soon disappeared through the heavy wooden front door.

Betty wondered why he had bothered to tell her that he was invading the earl's home. Then she realized that he had such a high opinion of himself he felt entitled to boast that he could do whatever he chose, even if it wasn't really good manners to do it. He knew the countess. Therefore, he could enter the house at will.

What a dislikable young man, she thought. It wouldn't trouble me if he were shot as a burglar. Then she thought that in such an event, he might be said to have died for his art.

CHAPTER 2

THE OTHER guests were beginning to take their leave, although the young woman introduced as Chloe Waters seemed to be in no hurry to depart, having inappropriately placed herself firmly between David and Lys. Some girls never give up, Betty thought. Then Margaret swooped down and dislodged Chloe gracefully, so that the couple could drift away to the Priory to change into their traveling clothes for their honeymoon trip.

Margaret brought Chloe to Betty.

"Miss Waters has invited us to Figge Hall if we have time after we return from Italy," Margaret said. "It's a lovely old house."

"Margaret is in charge of my movements," Betty said. "I don't know that we'll be returning to England on this trip."

Chloe pouted, or perhaps her petulant expression was normal for her. "I've asked David and that . . . that barmaid to visit later in the summer. Daddy would be delighted to see him. I thought we could have a garden party in his honor. I don't suppose he'll come though."

"No," Margaret said firmly. "I think not."

"Ah, Margaret . . ." Betty began uneasily. "I wonder if it is all right that that artist, Benedict, is roaming around the house in search of a painting he wants to see."

"*Not* all right, as far as I am concerned," Margaret said. She summoned the new butler with a wave of her hand.

"Yes, m'lady?" Simmons was a good-looking young man who took great care of his body. He looked very strong.

"There is a man in the house who was a guest at the wedding—dark hair, none too well dressed. He claims to be looking at a painting. The Holbein probably. I wish you would find him and gently escort him out. He's in the Great Hall or the library. I know nothing about him, and all of the wedding gifts are on display in the Great Hall. Some lovely silver pieces . . ."

"I understand, m'lady. I assigned Potts to keep guard over the gifts during the ceremony and reception and buffet, so the young man won't be able to remove anything."

"Excellent, but I would still like him out of the house."

"I'll see to it at once." Simmons moved off purposefully, and the set of his broad shoulders suggested that expulsion would soon be accomplished.

Suddenly David and Lys appeared in the doorway, Lys dressed casually in beige slacks and a matching tailored silk jacket. As the newlyweds awaited the horse-drawn carriage that had brought the bride to the church for the ceremony and would now take them away, Betty saw Simmons and Benedict emerge behind them.

Simmons gripped Benedict's arm firmly and guided him behind a tall hedge, away from the bride and groom. Benedict appeared to be protesting his innocence, but Simmons paid him no heed. The couple didn't notice him, and then an old man—Betty remembered that he was Potts, the family retainer who had driven them from London to the Priory—struggled out with several handsome traveling cases and piled them on the steps. The remaining guests moved closer, and Lys tossed her rose-laden bouquet into the crowd. Chloe Waters had pushed forward to catch it, which she did with a smug look. David tossed the bride's lacy garter, and it was caught by one of the small boys who had participated in the wedding.

He did not seem to know what to do with it. Lester Flood, having regained reasonable humor, chuckled at the sight of the boy gingerly holding the garter between thumb and forefinger. Behind him, Phyllis was engaged in a head-to-head conversation with Benedict Howe, who had emerged from behind the hedge where Simmons had deposited him.

The photographers shot more pictures as the carriage, pulled by a distinctly senior horse, moved sedately along the curving drive and stopped in front of David and Lys. When the luggage was loaded, they drove away.

"Where will they honeymoon?" Betty asked.

"Up to London for the night," Margaret said.

"And no, they won't travel there by horse and carriage; that's just for show. Then they're off to somewhere warm and unclouded. The South of France, or Italy perhaps—they didn't tell me exactly where—but the Amalfi coast is nice. They're not going to Rome, I believe. Otherwise, David would have arranged a meeting with us."

"It was a perfect day," Betty said, as Phyllis joined them, abandoning Benedict for the moment.

"*Wasn't it divine!!!*" Phyllis had removed her too-large hat and was fanning herself. "Lys looked lovely, every inch a countess, and David is such a handsome boy. And I can't thank you enough, Margaret, for sending Benedict to us." She beamed over her shoulder at him. "He has *wonderful* ideas. He's going to start on a lovely big painting for the drawing room as soon as he gets back from Italy. And I think—" Phyllis giggled girlishly. "—I'll have him do my portrait as a gift for Lester's birthday."

"Nothing naughty, I hope," Margaret said absently, and didn't notice, although Betty did, that Phyllis blushed.

"Certainly not," Phyllis said, "although he is an attractive young man in a bohemian sort of way. And very concerned about the taste of his clients. He wanted to know if we had any particular style in mind for the big painting in the drawing room. I'm going to enjoy working with him. Ooo-hoo! Lester, I'm over here."

Before they could be accosted by Lester Flood, Margaret reminded Betty that Potts was waiting to show her the grounds. "He has so much to do today, I don't like to keep him hanging about." Margaret guided Betty toward a nearby formal garden. They paused to wave to the duke and duchess, who were entering their sedate black Rolls.

"I don't remember any such appointment with Mr. Potts," Betty said, "but if you were escaping the Floods, I'd say you did a smooth job of it." She stopped walking and cocked her head. "Curious, though."

"What?"

"I find it curious that Mr. Howe, who claims that his great art is unappreciated by the critics and the public, would be willing to adapt said art to any style preferred by people such as the Floods."

"No doubt he feels that the Floods would also be unable to appreciate his work," Margaret said, but she understood Betty's puzzlement. "I don't want to think anymore about Benedict Howe. I didn't find him likable. I especially dislike the idea of his wandering through the Priory without a responsible adult on hand.

"Well," she added briskly, "even if Potts is not waiting for you specifically, I'm sure he'd be delighted to give you a tour. He's very proud of his handiwork at the Priory, and he does have a gift for making things grow. The flowers decorating the church came from our gardens. Potts was up at dawn to cut them. Tilda the maid arranged them; she has a gift for it. Lys's bouquet was by a very elevated London florist who does the bouquets for the very best weddings. You can't have a good wedding without her."

Soon Betty and Potts were marching through the thick grass of the Priory's centuries-old lawn, inspecting lush flowerbeds, and Betty was confessing to Potts her personal lack of success with gardens.

"Nothing to it, ma'am," Potts said. "Kindness, water, and a bit of fertilizer do the trick. Roses want special attention, of course, especially in our climate. Weeding is important, but it's a real chore for me nowadays. I used to have Toby Mills as my right hand, but he's gone off to those Americans. Says the shouting gets him down, but the pay is good. So I got me some boys from the village to help. It's getting hard for me to go down on my knees to do proper weeding.

"Now, Lord Brayfield has given me permission to put in a little pond in the south garden. I've always fancied having a few koi to look after. Lovely fish, they are, and they get to know you because you feed them. I'd put in some nice orange nasturtiums near the pond to match the fish. And tulips of the right color in the spring. Oh, won't it be a treat to watch my fish."

"It sounds lovely to me," Betty said politely, although she had no particular liking for bug-eyed fish with flowing fins.

Margaret joined them and gazed off at the empty meadows. "I certainly do miss seeing the cows out there."

"It was a pity indeed when they carted them away," Potts said. "The foot-and-mouth was a terrible thing. The cattlemen are all at loose ends now, spending too much time in Jimmy Grant's pub and wasting whatever money they have left on too many pints. If we don't get restocked soon, Jimmy is going to be so busy, he'll need the countess back behind the bar of The Riming Man to help out." He seemed amused to picture the Countess of Brayfield serving up drinks to her estate's laborers, even though she'd spent most of her adult years doing just that.

"She always enjoyed being a barmaid," Margaret said. "Betty, you can continue on with Potts if you'd like, but I want a word with you first." Potts moved away, and Margaret continued, "I'm so grateful that you warned me about Benedict being in the house. Simmons said he found him surreptitiously sketching—copying—the Holbein. Daddy loaned it out only once, years ago, for a major exhibit in London. He never cared to have people gawking at it.

"It's a portrait of a Priam ancestor. I'll show it to you later. And there's a picture in the library from the school of Botticelli. I do hope Howe didn't get into that room to attempt to copy it. Now I want to ring Paul in America on the urgent matter of Benedict Howe. It's just after noon in New York, and I hope to catch him before he leaves for a job interview or the like."

Prince Paul Castrocani had an aversion to working, or perhaps lacked the talent, and preferred to live on his mother's generous allowance. Alas, Carolyn Sue and her latest husband, Benton Hoopes, were increasingly reluctant to support Paul, so he was constantly attempting to find a job for which he was suited, seldom with much success. Margaret hoped that she could devise a plausible and satisfying story for his father about his employment status.

"Mrs. Domby will serve us tea in half an hour or so, but I'll join you after I've made my call. Potts, please show Miss Trenka to the tea table, and explain to Mrs. Domby that I won't be but a minute."

CHAPTER 3

BETTY WONDERED if she could eat another bite after the delicious canapes she'd been served and the generous buffet that had followed. Mrs. Domby, in consultation with the new mistress of the house, had decided against a sit-down meal on this surprisingly warm summer day, and consequently Betty's knees ached from the long day of standing. She'd welcome a comfortable chair somewhere in the shade. So she gladly followed Potts through the thick grass to a spot under a shady tree and sank into a cushioned chair with relief.

Potts took himself off on his own business while Margaret made her way into Priam's Priory and stood for a moment gazing down the long hallway toward the Great Hall. How she wished that Wally, the old black Lab, was still alive to drag himself over to sniff her hand and lean against her legs. But Wally had passed on to his celestial kennel shortly after her last visit to the Priory several years before.

David had replaced him with a rambunctious golden retriever named Mitford, of all things, because of his fondness for the writing of Nancy and

Jessica and the antics of their sisters. Wally had had
the run of the house, but Mitty, whom she had only
met on this visit, was forbidden to enter and spent
her days romping in the meadows, scattering pheas-
ants and terrifying bunnies.

Margaret entered the Great Hall and glanced at
the table gleaming with silver wedding gifts, then
at the dark paintings hanging on the walls. There
was the Holbein that Benedict Howe had been so
eager to view—a portrait of an early Priam who
bore an eerie resemblance to both her father and her
brother. Margaret loved the young man's blond
curls, his rich velvet tunic, the heavy gold chain
around his neck, and the massive ring set with a
dark stone on his finger. The ring still existed on the
floor above, safely locked in the lump of a safe from
which Lys had unearthed the family tiara for the
wedding ceremony. It was there, that is, unless the
financial travails besetting the Priory estates had
forced David to sell it. But surely he wouldn't take
such a step without informing her.

She glanced again at the portrait and remembered
sitting on the floor as a child, imagining the young
Earl of Brayfield as he attended Queen Elizabeth at
her splendid court or welcomed her to the Priory as
she made her way around her realm, sponging off
her subjects.

The portrait of Margaret's Priam ancestor was
not her favorite, however. The Indian miniatures of
Mughal emperors, fighting elephants, dark-eyed
princesses, scrawny saints, lovers in fantastic gardens, and leaping tigers had enchanted her as a

child. Some hung in her old bedroom, with a few of
the most precious here in the Great Hall above the
linen-draped table covered with the wedding gifts.
Others were carefully kept in a thick leather port-
folio in the library. All of them had been brought to
the Priory by her father's brother, Uncle Lawrence,
who had served his country and the Raj faithfully as
a member of the Indian Civil Service.

Her greatest favorites, though, were the luminous
paintings of the Pre-Raphaelites, also seldom viewed
by outsiders and even more rarely photographed.
Before the turn of the century, her grandfather had
fallen in with Dante Gabriel Rossetti, Edward
Burne-Jones, Ford Madox Brown, and the rest. And
since he had a substantial inheritance, he helped
them financially, receiving as repayment paintings of
femmes fatales and legendary women with stars in
their hair.

As a teenager, Margaret had wished that she had
been blessed with the thick, curly hair and full lips
of a Pre-Raphaelite woman, been allowed to dress
in damask robes and thus been able to ensnare the
strongest-minded men by her dangerous beauty
alone. She preferred the painting *La Belle Dame
sans Merci* by Rossetti to the undoubtedly more
valuable Rembrandt painting of a plump, gnomish
Dutch gentleman that held pride of place in the hall.

Any of these pictures might have been the one
Benedict wanted to see, although finer examples of
the artists hung in museums and galleries all over
the world. What was his game? She hurried out
of the room to the cubbyhole in the hallway where

the telephone, with a comfortable armchair and a little table furnished with pen and paper for notes, awaited.

Paul's phone in the United States rang several times before he answered.

"It's Margaret."

"You're not already in Italy, are you, *bella?*"

"No, we're still here at the Priory. The wedding's just over. It was perfect. I'll tell you all about it when I get back. But I wanted to ask you something about one of the guests. A young man named Benedict Howe."

"Ben? Is he still alive, and what was he doing at your brother's wedding?"

"What do you mean by that? Of course he's alive, he's a young man. He says he knows you."

"What I mean is, yes, I know him, and no reasonably civilized person ought to have him in socially. I should have thought his history would have caught up with him by now, and some angry gentleman would have terminated him."

"Ah, I see. He's a womanizer, then? Perhaps my brother is right to be jealous. Lys, his new wife, knew Benedict at Oxford."

"Womanizer? Not exactly, or only on occasions when it is to his benefit. I had the impression that he preferred men to women. No, the angry gentleman would be someone he had cheated or made a fool of. I myself was even a minor victim of old Ben's machinations. He persuaded me to do something I knew was not right. Ben's dishonest in a variety of ways, but he can be charming. I know he once charmed my mother, who is no fool. I used to see him at the nightclubs in Rome and holding court at cafes on the Via Veneto. He liked to say he was an artist, but the only art of his I ever saw were drawings he'd copied from famous works around Rome. They were quite convincing replicas—almost forgeries. He claims that copying was the traditional way for young artists to learn the techniques of the masters.

"I remember he once boasted that he and one of his mates had sold some of his copies to gullible tourists as the real thing. One of his chums was an English boy who had a reputation as a gigolo. Ben was also said to do business with a rather sinister art dealer, probably in the matter of his forgeries. Still, he seemed to know a great deal about art. It must have been ten years ago, before my parents divorced, but I haven't forgotten him. I had no idea he'd studied at Oxford. For some reason he never advertised the fact. It probably wouldn't have suited the poor, struggling artist image that he cultivated."

"He says he is to be in Rome when Elizabeth and I are there, and wants to see a painting your father owns."

"Margaret, be very wary of Howe. And I do not believe my father cares to open his home so the curious can view a few unauthenticated old masters. My father once turned away Bernard Berenson himself, who was greatly displeased. He wouldn't hesitate to turn Howe away. He already has."

"I see. I appreciate the information." She then

told him about Benedict's visit to the Priory's Great Hall to look at the Priam pictures.

"Are all the paintings still in place?" Paul asked anxiously. "I think he would happily cut them out of their frames."

"All there. Most of them are too large to carry off, even when rolled up, without someone noticing. He's an art thief then?"

"I do not know that for a fact, but I believe he does not hesitate to take whatever he wants. During our brief acquaintance, there were occasions when objects disappeared without explanation. Small things. A valuable pen, a bit of jewelry, a pretty American tourist's passport and wallet. Howe liked to live well, so I believe he stole things when he needed money. I can't say that he was the culprit, but he'd always been recently around when the loss was discovered. Then suddenly his pockets would be stuffed with lire, and he'd hint that the dealer I mentioned had paid him well for forgeries. Of course, he didn't actually say they were forgeries, just hinted at that.

"Promise to warn my father about him; he met Howe years ago but may not remember. Benedict once accompanied me to the villa, claiming to be interested in sampling the modest vintage my father produces. It is not very good, so the story was an excuse to get near my father's paintings. Instead he got near Carolyn Sue, who was strangely taken with him. Of course, she was bored living at the villa and had run out of ways to change things around, much to my grandmother's disgust. Oh, the quarrels Nonna and my mother used to have over matters as simple as planting flowers of a different color in the urns along the drive."

"I promise to take care," Margaret said. "Elizabeth and I are off to London tomorrow for a bit of sightseeing. We had no time before the wedding, only enough to find me a hat. Then it's on to Rome."

"Be sure to tell my father that I am doing well in New York. Whatever you may think, I believe such news will comfort him in his old age. Ah . . . Margaret . . ." Paul said hesitantly, "you'll probably be meeting Nonna, my grandmother. You may find her difficult. She's been a little crazy—*pazza*, the peasants say—since the war. The Germans had their headquarters at Frascati, which isn't far from Villa Carolina. Wartime was very bad for her. My grandfather died then; the Germans executed him. Later, when my father was grown and he married my mother, he sent Nonna to a sanitarium in Switzerland, but she came home from time to time to duel with Carolyn Sue. Now she's back at Villa Carolina permanently, living with my father."

"Villa Carolina?"

"My sentimental father renamed it for my mother, which displeased my grandmother very much. There's another, more famous Villa Carolina in the vicinity. Be sure to go to the right one. Nonna didn't get on with Carolyn Sue, who had unacceptable ideas of how the villa should be decorated and managed, and the family's palazzo, Palazzo Ingranno, which is mostly abandoned now. You know how bossy my mother is. She must have her way. Surely Carolyn Sue told you about Nonna."

"Not much. Only that she had a difficult mother-in-law, who was a bit unstable."

"Nonna is very possessive about the villa and palazzo, but she's a game old girl. Very social in her day, and a great beauty once, I'm told. She was always just an odd old lady to me, always dressed in black as a widow must be. She must be close to ninety now. Just don't overexcite her or give her the idea that you're another foreign woman with designs on my father. Enjoy your visit with the old boy."

Margaret replaced the receiver. She was disappointed that Paul had not mentioned Sam De Vere or conveyed a message from him. She'd spoken to De Vere briefly before departing, but he hadn't seemed to care much about where she was going. Perhaps she shouldn't have gone on so enthusiastically about the visit to Paul's father. Sam wasn't blind. He was aware that Paul was attractive to ladies, and that his father probably was as well. But De Vere wasn't at all a jealous man.

Then she frowned. She'd never had the impression that Prince Aldo was in the midst of "old age." But of course Carolyn Sue was in her late fifties and as well-preserved as endless money allowed. Her former husband was older, but by how much, Margaret didn't know. She imagined Aldo as a slightly older version of Paul, dark and handsome and utterly charming. She hoped that she and Elizabeth would not be greeted at the gates of the villa by a gray-haired, doddering ancient, with his crazy mother trailing after him.

Then she turned her thoughts to Benedict Howe. Artists were often—or usually—poor, and obliged to seize any opportunity for cash. She decided to have Potts or Mrs. Domby check the wedding gifts against the list of items received to be certain that nothing had gone missing.

She hastened back to the lawn to join Betty for tea. Mrs. Domby's culinary creativity was taking a rest, since tea consisted merely of little sandwiches and cakes left over from the reception. One of the Priory's beautiful Georgian silver tea sets had appeared, and Betty was chatting warily with two of the children who had been in the wedding party, who were staying the night at the Priory with their parents. One of them was a distant Priam relative, but Margaret wasn't certain about the connection. The important thing, after all, had been to snare some children willing to dress up and behave. In this, Lys had succeeded admirably.

"Gillian tells me she is very clever, already able to read almost anything," Betty said to Margaret. "Anthony is keen on what he calls Manchester United. I think it must have something to do with sports."

"Yes, it's a football team. Soccer. Run along, children. We need to talk about grown-up things."

They ran. "I do find children difficult," Betty said. "They talk about matters I don't understand, and then come up with the most amazing statements. Gillian told me that the 'noisy American lady'—that would be your Mrs. Flood, I hope, because I certainly haven't been noisy—was seen 'leaning on the nasty man.' Perhaps she meant Mr. Flood, but I doubt it. From a child's point of view, I think only Benedict Howe could be deemed nasty among the guests here."

"Leaning? As in feeling faint, or snuggling up romantically? Or just what?"

"I cannot say," Betty said. "It has been a tiring day, and I can't think."

"Perhaps you'd care to lie down for a time. I don't think Mrs. Domby is planning any more food for today, although Tilda will bring you something if you wish."

"I suppose I ought to rest. Although my bed is . . . is a bit of a trial, even if a queen did sleep there."

"We haven't wanted to change anything since Elizabeth's visit here," Margaret said. "Not even the mattress. I could have you moved to another room."

"Don't trouble. I can manage. When I was young, I once had to give up my bed to my brother and sleep on the floor until Pop could afford to buy a new one for me. We're leaving tomorrow anyhow."

"About ten, I think, when Potts has finished his morning chores. Breakfast at seven, if you're awake."

Betty didn't bother to tell her that she'd never stayed in bed beyond seven-thirty in her life.

At the door of the Priory, Betty looked back over

the lawns where the shadows were lengthening as the last of the sun disappeared behind a clump of tall and ancient oaks. A few estate laborers were gathering up the odds and ends of trash left by the guests, all of whom had long since departed. Mrs. Domby carried the silver tea service around to the back of the house to some hidden kitchen entrance.

"What a lovely day it's been," Betty said. "Thank you for inviting me. To think I almost decided to back out, but my friend Ted Kelso shamed me into changing my mind."

"I always feel renewed when I come home. And I think the duke was quite taken with you," Margaret said. "The next time you visit me in New York, you can give Terry Thompson a thrill by describing your friendship with the Duke of Kent."

"If I start dropping names like that, she'll definitely be convinced that I really am some sort of Czech nobility and will expect me to wear a tiara. No, I don't want to be mistaken for someone I definitely am not."

Margaret scanned the star-splattered sky and the peaceful countryside.

"Elizabeth," she whispered urgently. "Is that someone lurking down there at the edge of the drive?"

Betty squinted in the direction she indicated. Her sight was imperfect in spite of her thick glasses, but she could discern a dark shape on the white gravel. A man, she thought. But he wasn't really lurking. Rather he was standing casually, and he looked as though he was scanning the drive as it wound down the hill to the road that led to the village of Upper Rime.

"It seems to be a man, maybe someone waiting for a ride that hasn't appeared yet."

"Toby!" Margaret headed toward the laborer who had faced Lester's wrath and spoke to him. He quickly trotted off toward the lurker. Margaret rejoined Betty. "We don't like strangers hanging about, especially with all those lovely gifts on display. Simmons is so new that I don't altogether trust him to lock up properly, and Potts is getting on in years. Not really up to confronting a burglar."

Toby rejoined them. "Says he was at the wedding and is waiting for a lift. A Mr. Howe, he says he is. Says you know him, m'lady."

"I do. Thank you for checking on him, Toby. I didn't know you were back with us. I thought you'd gone to the Floods on a permanent basis."

"Potts asked me to help out today, so I came back to the Priory for a day. That Mr. Flood is a terror to work for over at Rime Manor. I'm sorry I left the Priory. Does business by way of shouting, he does." Toby sounded disgusted. "I'll keep an eye on the lad there, and if he hangs about too long, I'll run him off the estate."

"It's curious, don't you think? Who could be giving him a lift?"

"He told me that he was off to London some time ago," Betty said, "and all the Londoners are gone now."

"He didn't say, ma'am," Toby said. "He just said he'd be staying in the neighborhood for the night, and he'd be away soon."

Just then, headlights appeared through the trees at the bottom of the hill, and soon a sleek, dark car stopped and Benedict Howe got in.

"Looks to be a Jaguar," Margaret murmured. She'd been away for so long that she wasn't familiar with the kind of cars the local people drove, but surely no one in Upper Rime was prosperous enough to own a Jaguar. Even Jimmy Grant, with a monopoly in the pub market, couldn't afford such an auto. Then it struck her.

"It must be the Floods he's staying with." They could afford a Jaguar. She was only surprised that it wasn't a Rolls or a Bentley. "How odd that they invited him."

"Maybe he wants to study their house to determine what sort of painting he'll do for them," Betty said. "I didn't like him much. But remember what Gillian said about Mrs. Flood leaning on the nasty man. Is there an illicit romance budding? In that event, I don't imagine Mr. Flood will welcome him as an overnight guest."

"But Phyllis will. Howe did mention that she was an attractive woman in need of distraction. It seems Howe has decided to distract her, and she fell for it. I've never credited Phyllis with much sense. Or Lester either, since he bought Rime Manor in the first place and has undertaken its renovation. The cost must be horrendous and the upkeep will be continuous. The manor's leaking roof is legendary around here. No one has ever been able to fix it.

"Daddy spent a fortune bringing in the best the building trades have to offer, but to no avail. So he gave up, as my ancestors did over the centuries. In fact, I can show you where the roof was noted in estate records going back to the seventeen-hundreds. We can only hope Benedict's painting will be placed where it's well protected. Well, Benedict's adventures in art and romance have nothing to do with us. Let's go in. It's getting chilly."

CHAPTER 4

Betty was grateful to get into the warmth of the Priory. Who would have believed that a warm June day would turn into such a cool evening? Although Queen Elizabeth's mattress was lumpy, she looked forward to lying down.

"If you're not too tired, Betty, I want to show you our book about the Priory's ghosts. There are two of them, a nun from the days when this really was a religious establishment and a murdered wife we call the Gray Lady. Everyone who sees one or the other is required to record the sighting in the book."

"Real ghosts?"

"As real as they get. I'm afraid I can't promise a sighting for you. They keep their own schedule, and can't be summoned at will. But they do tend to appear when there's a death in the vicinity."

"Then I hope they stay away," Betty said. "I don't want my visit spoiled by a dead person."

"I wouldn't worry. There's nobody in the house now who appears on the brink of death, unless, of course, someone has murder on his or her mind."

She led Betty down the long hallway and opened

the door to the library. All Betty could see in the dark room were the shapes of big chairs and sofas, and bookcases on every wall stretching from floor to ceiling. Margaret switched on a lamp near a cluster of chairs, and Betty saw the gleam of gold lettering on the spines of thousands of leatherbound books.

"Have a seat," Margaret said, "and I'll find the ghost book."

Betty sank into a puffy chair, glad to be off her feet, and looked about the room more closely. Heavy dark drapes covered the windows, and on a far wall between two bookcases, she could just make out a portrait in an elaborate gilded frame of a seated woman dressed in a fanciful gown.

"Margaret, would that be the Botticelli?"

Margaret looked up from the floor where she was kneeling to examine a shelf of books.

"And you told me you knew nothing about art. Yes, it's labeled 'school of Botticelli,' an imitation that one of my ancestors brought back from his Grand Tour of the continent. Quite valuable, I understand, because of its age if nothing else, but we had an expert in to examine it. He concluded it was a copy, but from the right era. I'm glad Benedict didn't try to see it as well as the Holbein, but then we've never advertised its existence.

"We have an album of old master drawings here in the library, too. Howe could easily have rolled one up and taken it away, but we don't talk about those either. A lot of old families have similar—and much better—collections of drawings. The Devonshires, and the Queen, of course, at Windsor Castle. And I heard that a Michelangelo drawing was recently discovered at Castle Howard.

"David looks at our album from time to time, just in case he recognizes something as a real treasure. He never has, and he even had that expert take a look. He was not impressed. Ah, here it is."

She lifted a thick book from the shelf, carried it to Betty, and placed it on the low table in front of her.

"Here's the last sighting that I was involved in," Margaret said. "The Maharani of Tharpur was murdered in a passageway on the side of the house a few years ago, and there was another death a day or two later. The ghosts were wandering around both times." She turned the page. "Here's the very last one, just two months after the Maharani died, when I was back in New York. David claims he saw the nun in the white room that used to be the Priory refectory and is now his private lair. Shortly thereafter, Wally died." Betty looked puzzled. "Wally was the family dog. A lovely creature, but very, very old and very special to me. Nothing mysterious. It was time for him to go."

"Perhaps your nun was a Franciscan, and, like Saint Francis, had a special affinity to animals." Betty turned the silky old pages of the ghost book. "I see that your servants encountered the ghosts frequently over the years."

"And largely left our employ soon after. However, Mrs. Domby is quite strong-minded and has been known to clap her hands sharply to dismiss them. They don't *only* appear at the time of a death, I hasten to add. I think they enjoy startling people, although reports of the Gray Lady indicate that she's a sad-looking apparition, still grieving over the fact that her husband murdered her some centuries ago."

"Do they visit the Queen's Bedroom, I wonder?"

"No sightings reported there. I think you need not worry. Anyhow, they're quite harmless—just indistinct shapes that hover about for a time and then vanish."

"Oh, but I'd like to see a ghost," Betty said. "It would be a wonderful tale to tell Ted Kelso." She wondered how his treatment was progressing and resolved to write to him soon.

"Then I hope you get your wish," Margaret said. "I think I'll go to my bed now. This wedding has exhausted me. You can stay here as long as you like. Simmons will see to the lights and locking up."

"I'll come upstairs with you. I'm not sure of the way to my room, and I'd hate to spend the night wandering about lost like one of your ghosts."

They made their way to the grand staircase leading to the upper floors. A few faint lights were burning in wall sconces, but the stairs were in shadow. Margaret touched a switch on the wall and a chandelier high above them flickered on, but it shed little useful light. Betty clutched the polished bannister as she mounted the stairs carefully. How awful it would be to topple over and break a hip in a strange country. Then Margaret, a step or two ahead of her, stopped abruptly. All Betty heard was a deep sigh before Margaret reached back and took Betty's free hand.

"Look. Up there at the landing."

From descending the stairs that morning Betty remembered that a short flight from the floor above ended in a landing, and then a second flight, at right angles to the first, led to the ground floor. When she squinted through the murky darkness toward the landing, she thought—imagined?—that she saw the hazy shape of a woman in a long gray dress hovering in the shadows.

"Is it . . . ?"

"Yes," Margaret whispered. "The Gray Lady." As Betty watched, a little clutch of nervousness swept through her—after all, how often does one see a real ghost?—and the figure gradually became indistinct, until it was merely a grayish cloud. Then it slowly dissipated and was gone.

Margaret began to climb the stairs again, rather bravely, Betty thought, as she tried to remember every detail so that she could recount it clearly to Ted.

"You won't be afraid to be alone in the Queen's Bedroom, will you?" Margaret asked. "You can see she's harmless."

"I'll be all right," Betty said. "I've faced live murderers; I can handle a wispy little ghost."

Margaret guided her to her bedroom door and opened it, then turned on the lights to reveal the high canopied bed. The maid had turned down the red coverlet and closed the red curtains. There was a carafe of water on the bedside table, and a plate of chocolate-covered biscuits, and even a fresh bouquet of white flowers in a crystal vase. The maid had also packed her suitcase in preparation for the morning's departure, leaving it open so that Betty could pick out her traveling clothes and tuck in any odds and ends.

"Don't wear anything too fancy for the trip to London. Be comfortable. I'll see you at breakfast. Now I have to record our sighting of the ghost."

"Should I add my signature?" Betty asked.

"Don't trouble about it tonight. You can do it in the morning before we leave."

Margaret dutifully descended again, wrote out and dated the visit of the Gray Lady on David's wedding day, then replaced the volume on the bottom shelf. She noted with interest that there was a large gap in the row of old books, as though one had been removed and not replaced. These were bound volumes of old estate records, some going back to the sixteenth century when the Priory had first come into Priam hands. Perhaps David had been giving Lys a lesson in estate history.

"Ooof!" On her way out of the library, Margaret stumbled over an open book lying on the floor behind an easy chair. She picked it up and carried it to the table to examine it. It was a thick volume bound in dark green leather, and the front cover was stamped in gold with the Priam crest of three turreted towers.

It was one of the earliest estate books, but curiously, it appeared that several pale gray or greenish blank pages at the end had been neatly sliced away. Very curious. She didn't understand, but she replaced the book on the shelf, intending to ask David or the servants about it later. Thinking hard, Margaret went up to her own room, a comfortable, feminine place in contrast to Betty's overbearingly royal room.

Betty was so weary that the lumpy mattress didn't keep her awake, and before she knew it, morning had arrived, and Tilda the maid was opening the red curtains and setting a cup of tea on the bedside table.

"Lady Margaret was up early to go riding," Tilda said. "She said to tell you that she'd be back before seven-thirty to join you for breakfast. And won't it be quiet here with his lordship off on his honeymoon? The new Lady Priam is going to be a treat to work for. Before I came to work here, I used to help out in the kitchen of The Riming Man, and she was so kind. Of course, I don't really remember the old earl and Lady Margaret's mother—she died before I came to the Priory—although I used to see them when I was a child.

"The earl and the countess would have a garden fete for all the village children on May Day. We had a Maypole and sweets and ever so many good things. The present earl hasn't held a fete since his parents died, and weren't the children disappointed. But I wager that Lys—her ladyship, that is to say—will see to it next year. If I have to, I'll remind her, but of course she used to come to the fetes when she was little. She won't have forgotten."

Tilda paused to straighten an item of clothing in Betty's suitcase that had been shifted as she looked for something to wear today.

"Thank you for doing my packing," Betty said kindly. "It's a chore I hate."

Then she wondered if she should leave Tilda some of the odd English coins she'd acquired. She decided that she should. It might give the girl a different impression of Americans than the Floods represented.

At the thought of them, Betty remembered Benedict Howe and wondered exactly what he was up to. She couldn't help thinking that he would come to a bad end, like the stock man at Edwards & Son who had poached the fiancée of another fellow in the warehouse, who in turn had broken the poacher's nose, two ribs, and several teeth. Stealing was wrong, but Howe was not her concern. She chose navy slacks and a flowered shirt for the drive to London, comfortable shoes, of course, and a cardigan sweater in case the day turned cool. As soon as Tilda left, she dressed, and repinned her long, thick hair on top of her head and was ready for the day.

CHAPTER 5

BETTY HAD filled her plate with eggs, ham, and toast from the dishes set out on a long sideboard in the dining room when Margaret burst into the room, out of breath and clearly excited.

"You'll never guess," she said.

Betty found a seat at the dining table. "You went riding and decided to pass by the Floods' place, and you found that something had happened in the night."

"How . . . how did you know?"

"It seemed inevitable. I remember a poacher. I mean, a man who poached another man's woman. Anyone dead?"

"No, thank goodness, but the place is in an uproar. The village constable is there. Word spread fast because several villagers were gawking outside the hedges."

"Well, then. What happened?"

"An as-yet-unknown person shot a gun into the drawing room as Mrs. Flood and Benedict were having a quiet evening drink. Shot was wild and nobody was hurt. Well, Benedict was apparently

60

nicked by a bullet and a standing lamp was some-what damaged, but all's well that ends well."

"Was Benedict the target or was it Mrs. Flood?"

Margaret shrugged. "He was the one who was in-jured."

"Where was Mr. Flood when this occurred?" Betty continued.

"I don't know for certain. The constable was closed-mouthed about the affair and was busy see-ing that Benedict got patched up. A bit of blood, but nothing serious. Phyllis was hysterical. Lester was stamping around denying everything and accusing Howe of attacking him. Betty, what are you think-ing?"

"I was merely wondering if more 'leaning' was going on in the absence of Mr. Flood, who might have gotten wind of it and decided to send everyone bolt upright with a random shot or two. Things like that do happen. I doubt that Phyllis was the shooter, and it couldn't have been Howe. It was definitely Lester."

"But how do you figure that?"

"Human nature is human nature. It's perfectly logical. Jealousy or pure irritation on Lester's part, or he might have been gallantly protecting his pos-session, which is more likely. So he decided to ter-minate the source of irritation by murdering Howe to keep him from his wife."

"I did manage a word with Howe while he was wincing in pain from his damaged shoulder. He claimed to have been discussing that silly portrait Phyllis wants when Lester burst in waving a weapon and threatening murder. Benedict said, 'I'm too clever to be murdered, and certainly not over a woman.' I didn't speak with the Floods.

"But people in England don't normally have guns, except for hunting, and I don't think Lester has become quite that Anglicized. I doubt that he was able to smuggle a revolver into the country. Airport security is fairly strict here, and boarding a plane in America with a gun is difficult if not impossible. Still, I could be wrong. It's not impossible to buy a handgun here, and you Americans are so keen on owning them. Not you, Elizabeth, but the likes of Lester Flood. He seems an ideal candidate to own a gun.

"I guess I'll have to wait for the gossip to bring me a hint of what actually transpired. Mrs. Domby scoops up village gossip as readily as she scoops up dustballs. My, this is good. I never found a decent English breakfast in all of New York."

"Mr. Howe seems to be a magnet for trouble," Betty said. "I wonder what his game really is."

"I think you're right," Margaret said, and Betty cocked her head questioningly. "It is some sort of game, and we don't know the rules yet." Then she told Betty about finding the book with missing pages the previous evening.

"Mr. Howe did have some time alone in the house," Betty said. "But you'd think he'd try to scamper off with something more valuable than a few sheets of old paper."

"Nobody gave him a chance. Or maybe old paper

is more valuable than we know. I think we'll try to avoid him in Rome."

Just then, they were joined by the other house-guests, Gillian and Anthony and their parents, who Betty recalled were named Charles and Margot something.

"Good morning, Margaret, Miss Trenka," Margot said. "Very nice do yesterday. I can see you were well trained by your mother, Margaret."

"I had nothing to do with the arrangements. The new countess was completely in charge."

"That bodes well for the future of the Priory," Charles said. "A good sensible woman at the reins. Old David couldn't manage the place alone, that's for sure. His head is off in the hunting field. I suppose he still rides with the hunt?"

"David would rather be on a horse than on the Concorde," Margaret said. "That or whispering sweet nothings to the dairy herd. I do hope it can be replaced soon." She still could not remember how she was related to this couple.

"Anthony, please do not play with your food," Margot said firmly. "Behave yourselves, both of you."

"But, Mummy . . ."

Margot silenced her son with a look, and breakfast proceeded calmly.

"Heard from Potts that there was a shooting in the neighborhood last night," Charles said. "Terrible thing, but I understand no one was injured, at least not seriously."

Margaret offered no response, but Charles wasn't through. "They're saying that someone—the un-speakable American fellow—took a shot at that layabout Benedict Howe. I remember when Howe was a chum of Nigel's. Now that was a pair for you. My mum finally wouldn't allow Howe in the house, even if Nigel was her stepson."

Ah, now Margaret had it. Charles's mother was Uncle Lawrence's second wife, now deceased like his first. That made him a relative of sorts by marriage only.

"I don't actually know Benedict," Margaret said. "I met him for the first time at the wedding. He's a university friend of Lys's."

"A bad lot all around. Take my advice, Margaret, and warn David that Benedict shouldn't be a wel-come guest, however friendly he and Lys are. We'd all be better for it if that clot Flood had finished him off," Charles said.

"Why do you so dislike Howe?" Margaret asked.

Charles looked at her as though it was obvious why no well-bred person would welcome him. "He's not our sort, is he? I don't buy the poor, working-class lad who pulls himself up out of the muck and makes good in an upper-class world. An artist in-deed. They're worse than an honest field laborer."

Charles's glaring class prejudice had perhaps been absorbed from his stepfather, Uncle Lawrence, the Lord of the Raj. Betty was studying Charles with great interest as though he were some exotic crea-ture in a zoo.

"My mum told me he'd nipped off with some of

Lawrence's valuable bits that he brought back from India," Charles continued gleefully, as though to prove that the working class could be counted on to behave in a typically uncivilized manner.

"I see. Did Uncle Lawrence ever get them back?"

"Nigel rescued them. His inheritance, after all, if he'd lived to enjoy it. And remember Lawrence's library? Not quite as grand as the one here at the Priory, but he had some nice volumes from here that were shared among the sons when your grandfather died. It seems that Howe actually made off with a couple of books. What was puzzling was that, although they were very old—fifteenth or sixteenth century, I believe—they were empty."

"Empty?"

"Blank, I mean. There were a few pages where someone was keeping a journal—possibly a courtier from Elizabeth's time, or even the Queen herself— but the rest of the pages were blank. Handwritten documents from the period must have some value, but there were rarer items in the library if Howe wanted something to turn into cash."

"Curious," Margaret said, and remembered the vandalized book in the Priory's own library. She needed to think more about all this. "It's been lovely to see you, Charles. The children were so well behaved during the ceremony, Margot. You must be proud of them."

"They're old hands at weddings," Margot said. "But they'll outgrow that role before long, and then they'll be getting ready for their own weddings. I say, Gillian is quite taken with your Miss Trenka. I thought at first she must have been a schoolmistress, she's so good with children, but she told me she was a retired businesswoman."

Even now, Betty was conversing quietly with the two children. Anthony was describing something with great animation, probably the feats of Manchester United players, in the belief that this older lady was well informed on the subject. Elizabeth Trenka posing as someone she was not.

"Miss Trenka and I must be off to London soon. Then we're on our way to Rome in a day or two." Potts appeared in the doorway. "Here's Potts. It must be time to leave. Betty, are you packed?"

"Yes, and Tilda was so helpful."

"Mummy, Mummy, Miss Betty saw the ghost last night." Gillian dashed to her mother. "When can I see it?"

"Ghosts don't appear on command, dear. But maybe you'll be lucky enough to see it someday, if Cousin David invites us to stay again."

Gillian pouted. She wanted the ghost now.

"But you promised to show us where you saw it." Anthony and Gillian took Betty's hands and gently pulled her toward the door.

"All right, but then I have to leave."

"There's plenty of time. Potts is always early," Margaret said. "Then sign the ghost book in the library. Bottom shelf. I'll have Simmons bring down our cases and put them in the car." Betty and the two children went off to view the staircase, and Margaret stepped outdoors to the drive to supervise the stowing of the luggage.

"Simmons, while you and the other servants are alone here until Lord Priam returns from his honeymoon, do not, under any circumstances, allow Benedict Howe into the house. Especially not into the Great Hall or the library. And it may be that Mr. or Mrs. Flood will give some pretext for wanting to enter. I don't want them in the house either."

"Certainly not, m'lady. No one will be allowed into the house unless the earl is at home. There. Everything is in the car, and here's Miss Trenka and Potts."

Gillian and Anthony hovered excitedly just inside the door as Betty joined Margaret in the Land Rover. Potts got behind the wheel and started the engine.

"Thank you for doing such a good job in handling the wedding," Margaret said to Simmons, who ducked his head modestly.

"Good-bye, children," Betty called. "Good ghost-hunting."

The car glided along the drive, down the hill to the main road. Betty took one look back at stately Priam's Priory, then watched the hedgerows slip by, and the green, green meadows empty of cows. Along the road to the village, Margaret pointed out the roof of Rime Manor. A police car was parked on the side of the road and a very young constable leaned on the bonnet. Potts slowed down and called out, "Catch the criminal yet, Dickon?"

The constable grinned. "Just domestic trouble, Potts. All well in hand."

As they drove along the High Street of Upper Rime, Margaret pointed out Jimmy Grant's The

Riming Man pub with a swinging sign outside showing a troubadour with a lute. "We'll visit a pub in London so you can get a feel for what they're like."

"I'm not much of a beer drinker," Betty said, "and I understand the English drink it warm."

"I'm sure we can find some chilled for you. We have enough American tourists to make cool, if not cold, beer available. Oh, and there's a wonderful Indian restaurant near the British Museum that I want to take you to. Very hot and spicy if you like it that way, or less so if you prefer. And Harrods' Food Hall, Buckingham Palace, and the National Portrait Gallery and the Tate if you want to get started on viewing art before we reach Rome. Tea at Brown's Hotel, of course. The Victoria and Albert Museum is a must; Westminster Abbey, too. Even the Tower of London if we have time. We probably won't have time for Kew Gardens, but it's one of my favorite places. The flowers will all be in bloom now."

"Whatever you think I'll enjoy. I've already had a marvelous time at the wedding, even down to those nice little children," Betty said. "I'm amazed that I got on with them so well. I'm not ordinarily fond of children."

"Perhaps they imagined you were somebody's grandmother, even their own. She died when they were just babies."

"The curse of mistaken identity again. Where will it ever end?"

CHAPTER 6

UPON REACHING London in an hour or so, Potts gave Margaret and Betty a brief tour, driving slowly through a crowded Piccadilly Circus, around Trafalgar Square, and down Pall Mall to the gates of Buckingham Palace. Then they caught a glimpse of Westminster Cathedral, and even the Houses of Parliament and the Thames. Finally Potts drove them past Harrods' green facade with its glittering display windows facing busy Brompton Road in Knightsbridge. He turned in to a cobblestone oval lined with three- and four-story Georgian brick buildings.

"Here we are, m'lady." The neat little building where they'd stayed on their arrival from America was a mansion converted to a series of flats for short-term rental to tourists and people in from the country who didn't wish to stay in a hotel.

"David and Lys stayed the night at the Hyde Park Hotel near the Knightsbridge tube station," Margaret said. "But I hope that by now they're well on their way out of the country. I wouldn't want to stumble over them while they're honeymooning." She rang the bell and the female concierge that Betty remembered from their previous visit welcomed them in, directing Potts to take the lift to the third floor with their luggage.

"We'll be here two nights this time," Margaret said. "Then we'll take the train from Victoria to Gatwick and catch our flight to Italy in the afternoon."

After they'd settled into the comfortable furnished flat, Margaret said, "What would you like to do now?"

Betty said thoughtfully, "I suppose I'd like to take a ride on the Underground—the tube, that is—since we didn't have a chance to do so before the wedding, although I'm a bit hungry."

"I have it," Margaret said. "We'll pop around to Beauchamp Place, only a block away. There are some nice little restaurants there. Then we'll stroll to the tube station, and go, oh, to Covent Garden and look around. I want to see a bookseller on Charing Cross Road. It's nearby. There's another fellow I might want to talk to at a gallery, but I can't remember the address—I should have remembered to ask David. Then we'll decide whether to have tea at Brown's Hotel today or tomorrow. If tomorrow, we'll stop at Harrods' Food Hall on our way back and get some food to prepare for dinner here in the flat. It has a microwave and everything we need."

"And I checked the bed in my room," Betty said. "Queen Elizabeth never slept here. It's too comfortable."

They set out soon afterward, following Margaret's proposed plan for lunch on Beauchamp

Place, Betty having stated her preference for tea at Brown's the next day.

It was another warm June day with no hint of London drizzle when Margaret and Betty went out to find some lunch and stroll to the tube station.

Soon they had finished lunch and were venturing down the escalators at the Knightsbridge station and boarding a train. "It's much nicer than the New York subway," Betty said, "although I don't frequent those subways as much as you probably do."

"Definitely nicer," Margaret said. "Here's our stop. It's just a short way to Charing Cross Road. If you like you can look in the bookstores; there are hundreds of them. I want to see Alistair Bottoms, who was an old friend of my father's. I hope he's still alive. I need information."

"About the pages stolen from the book, I assume," Betty said.

"Well, yes. How did you know?"

Betty shrugged. "I intuited. When something unusual was missing from its usual place at the office, I couldn't rest until I learned *why* it was missing, not just who took it. Could I join you?"

"Certainly. If he's there, Mr. Bottoms is a real Dickensian character, and he doesn't just know about books. He knows about everything."

Emerging from the Underground, the two made their way to Charing Cross Road, stopping to trail down short alleyways lined with bookstores, until Margaret found the place she was looking for: A. BOTTOMS RARE BOOKS AND PRINTS, ESTAB. 1934.

"I believe Mr. Bottoms's father had a shop

around here much earlier, and probably his grandfather before that, but Alistair moved some of his rarer books to the Priory when the bombing started during the Second World War. We never had a single bomb hit Upper Rime. I'm not speaking from personal knowledge. The war was over long before I was born, after my father came home from service in the Far East, but the older servants still talk about it. Potts told me that a German parachutist was captured near the village by some pitchfork-wielding farmers."

"All I remember about the war were the men in uniform and the neighbors' boys who didn't come home," Betty said. She didn't mention the handsome, recently discharged soldiers who were not interested in dating the awkward, too tall young woman she was then, or her father ranting, "If you can't manage to attract a lonely soldier, then there's no hope for you."

"Did you ever marry?" Betty asked suddenly as they were about to enter Mr. Bottoms's shop. Betty had never asked personal questions of Margaret, and she wondered how she would respond.

"I was married once, very briefly," Margaret said. She didn't seem troubled by the personal nature of the inquiry. "It was not a wise move. I even had a child, but she was born with severe handicaps and soon died. I see my former husband now and again. He's happily remarried, so I must not have done him much damage."

"My parents hoped I would marry, because that's the only life they could imagine for me, but I failed them in that, and had a good life in spite of a lack of a husband," Betty said, and they left it at that. Margaret pushed open the shop door and they entered the dim, cluttered interior as a little bell rang musically somewhere in the back.

No one was about, but after a few seconds, a large man with a bushy mustache emerged from behind a heavy curtain that served as the door to the back room.

"Lady Margaret, what a treat to see you after all this time," rumbled the man who must be Alistair Bottoms.

"And you, Mr. Bottoms," Margaret said. "I'm in need of some advice, and thought you might be able to help me. This is my friend, Elizabeth Trenka, from America."

"Madame, welcome to my shop. Let me just find a place for you to sit." He moved piles of old books from two rickety chairs, raising little clouds of dust, and gestured to them to sit. Betty sat gingerly on the edge of her chair and looked around at the tall bookcases crammed with battered volumes. There was a wooden bin that appeared to be stuffed with folders containing prints, and a truly remarkable antique cash register decorated with gold curlicues. The yellow glass eyes of a stuffed owl glared at them from atop the register.

"Now, what can I do for you? I don't have any special books in stock just now, but then, neither you nor your brother inherited the collecting bug from your esteemed father and grandfather. I hope you haven't come to sell me something from the Priory library. It would be a pity to extract anything, although I do understand that the economy of the country has been severely damaged by this disease that's going around among the livestock. I say, didn't I read in the papers that your brother was recently married?"

"Just yesterday, at the church in Upper Rime. That's why I'm back in England for a visit. You remember Jimmy Grant of The Riming Man, surely. It was his daughter that my brother married."

"Good old Jimmy. Of course I remember him. He came up to London with Potts during the war to help me crate some books to leave at the Priory. He was just a lad, but he worked hard.

"And Potts—is he still active?" He meant, of course, was he still alive.

"Potts is as busy as ever. I don't know what we'd do without him."

"Our time grows short, though," Mr. Bottoms said sadly. He clapped his hands on his plump thighs. "Now what is it I can do for you?"

"I'm not here to sell books," Margaret said, "but to ask a question. Have you ever heard of a young artist called Benedict Howe?"

The twinkle in Mr. Bottoms's eyes vanished and he drew his bushy brows together in a frown as he stroked his healthy mustache.

"I have heard the name, as it happens," he said slowly.

"In what connection, may I ask?"

"One or two unsavory matters. Your Mr. Howe has put one or two things over on one or another of my acquaintances in the collecting world. I would not care to say anything beyond that."

"One more question, then. What would Benedict Howe want with blank sheets of paper from one of our very old estate books?"

"How old?"

"Sixteenth or seventeenth century. The estate records were once just loose sheets, but my grandfather, I believe, had them nicely bound up in leather. Some of the volumes had unused paper at the end, and it appears that Mr. Howe managed to slice out a few sheets and make off with them. I was just curious."

"Hmm. Paper has been made in different ways over the centuries, and scientists are now easily able to determine when paper was made. I immediately suspect, Lady Margaret, that Benedict Howe needed old paper because he intends to forge old master drawings and pass them off, preferably with an expert's authentication, as the real thing for a lot of money. He'd need paper of the right age to do that. Any materials used for forgery—paper, canvas, wooden panels—have to be the right age for authentication."

"But surely he couldn't get away with it," Margaret said.

"My dear Lady Margaret, he could—and he has. I speak from personal experience."

CHAPTER 7

ALISTAIR BOTTOMS refused to give specific details of his dealings with Benedict Howe and merely warned Margaret to limit her association with him.

"Too clever for his own good. I hope he is not stopping in the vicinity of Priam's Priory," Mr. Bottoms said.

"I believe he has accepted a commission to do a painting for an American couple who recently purchased Rime Manor. It may be that he will paint elsewhere and merely deliver the finished work to them, but it's possible that he will work on the painting at the Manor. Unfortunately, David is away on his honeymoon, and Miss Trenka and I are departing for Rome in a day or two, so only the servants will be at the Priory for a few weeks. However, they have been warned not to allow Benedict Howe into the house."

"That's something," Mr. Bottoms said, but he seemed dejected. "I hope he has not mastered a burglar's skills. I cannot tell you how much trouble that young man caused. I suppose you still have that nice Holbein painting of your ancestor?"

"Hanging in the Great Hall, as always. It must be of the same era as the pages sliced out of the book."

"Very close. Howe could easily develop a so-called preliminary drawing of the portrait and pass it off as an authentic preliminary Holbein sketch of the young man. There's at least one such drawing in existence of a better-known Holbein portrait. I believe it belongs to the Queen and is stored at Windsor. However, a Holbein isn't worth what a Da Vinci or Michelangelo drawing would fetch. Raphael is another with a high value. Still, if Howe can pass it off, he'd make a tidy sum, and it's not likely he's going to stop with your comparatively unknown portrait. With a handful of sixteenth-century blank sheets of paper, he has a lot of options open." Mr. Bottoms frowned. "I have been given to understand that he has the ability to copy accurately enough to fool the experts. 'Forge' would be a more correct word, since he takes great pains to make the resulting work appear genuine. I've seen some of his works, and they certainly fooled me, although I'm no expert, merely somewhat knowledgeable."

"Now that you mention it," Margaret said, "our butler found him surreptitiously sketching the Holbein."

"There you have it. I'll keep my ears open for an announcement of a previously undiscovered Holbein drawing reaching the sale or auction market, and give a word of warning to whoever is offering it. Of course, some dealers might not care if they can get the right price for it."

"But surely dealers know about him and

wouldn't buy from him." Betty realized that it was provincial of her to be shocked that an illegal trade in forgeries was allowed to go on, but she was unsettled. At least it was only money and not murder.

"From what I've heard," Alistair said, "he has befriended certain experts who assist in authenticating the pictures, and he usually is clever about providing a provenance for them. That is where difficulties for the Priam could arise."

"But we would have nothing to do with forgery!"

"That young man could put himself and your family in an extremely precarious position. Forgery is a serious crime, and the bane of the art world. Most reputable dealers would prefer not to sell fakes to their clients. Of course some less honest dealers go to great trouble to authenticate doubtful works. We have to assume that if a forged Holbein drawing of your Priam ancestor appears, it will come with an apparently authentic provenance, namely the collection of the Earl of Brayfield.

"He owns the portrait, so it's logical that he would also have a preliminary drawing for it. If it's ever found out to be a fake, David will have to defend himself, and prove he did not connive with the forger. Not a pleasant prospect."

Mr. Bottoms heaved a great sigh, as if he was worn out by his long explanation. He leaned back in his chair and closed his eyes.

Margaret and Betty exchanged glances, then Margaret said, "I do appreciate the information, Mr. Bottoms. I recall that when I worked as an assistant to an oriental antiques dealer named Bedros

Kasparian, a very astute man, he was once fooled into acquiring a piece of jade that was supposed to be from the T'ang period. He quickly discovered that the carving was modern. I still remember his fury at being taken in by a forgery."

Bottoms nodded wearily.

"Thank you again for your help and advice. Miss Trenka and I ought to be leaving now."

He opened his eyes. "I will inform you or your brother if I hear anything about a Holbein. Safe journey to Italy. It's been years since I had a chance to travel."

Margaret and Betty stepped out into the bright sunshine and mixed with the crowd of book seekers on the pavement.

"Very informative," Betty said. "I suppose Mr. Howe learned about the importance of the paper's age while he was studying art history, and presumably he knows about using the right kind of ink or chalk or whatever to ensure that his drawings pass for the real thing."

"He's a menace, and I certainly hope he doesn't get David into trouble. Do you want to look in some of the bookstores, or perhaps window-shop on Regent Street?"

"I think," Betty said, "that I'd like to buy a few postcards. Ted Kelso will be expecting to hear from me."

"Simple enough. And why don't we take a quick look at the British Museum? Although 'quick' is not the way to see the museum. But the Elgin Marbles are wonderful, and we can also see the Rosetta

Stone and the Magna Carta, and the Sumerian gold objects. That area is quite interesting. There are plaques on the houses around Russell Square, showing where the Bloomsbury crowd used to live. Virginia Woolf and the rest."

So they found a black London cab and were whisked to the imposing front of the British Museum, where they spent the balance of the afternoon gazing at the Elgin Marbles in the big white room devoted entirely to the sculpted images of Greek gods and goddesses, wild-eyed horses, and the frieze that had once adorned the Parthenon. Betty found some postcards, and, when they left the museum, they rested on a bench in the green park in the middle of Russell Square while Betty wrote out a card to Ted. She did not mention the affair of Benedict Howe.

"The concierge at the flat will have stamps," Margaret said. "We'll go to Harrods now and find something for tea or supper, whichever you wish to call it."

Harrods' Food Hall intrigued Betty, who picked out some cheese seldom found in the United States, and a few other premade things that only needed heating.

"I used to love to buy Harrods' meat pies when I was stopping in London," Margaret said, "but I hesitate to eat British meat because of mad cow. Maybe I'm being silly, but I just can't bring myself to do it."

"Better careful than ill," Betty said.

Margaret bought some wine at the wine shop,

and they were soon back at the flat, toasting bread and cheese, and sipping their wine in front of the television set.

"Tomorrow in the morning, we'll go to the National Portrait Gallery, shall we? I confess that Mr. Bottoms has gotten me interested in portraits. It won't be a heavy-duty art visit, just a look around. Then we'll poke around Piccadilly Circus, or walk along the Strand and find a place for lunch—a light one, because I do intend to take you off to tea at Brown's Hotel in the afternoon. Maybe we'll get tickets for a play in the evening. Our flight is at one-thirty the next day, so we'll be at the Rome airport around five o'clock the day after tomorrow. I've arranged for a car to meet us at the airport, and we'll be at the Inghilterra an hour later if there's not too much delay at Immigration and Customs—although traffic in and around Rome is appalling. It's not really a three and a half hour flight. The continent is an hour ahead of us, so it's only two and a half hours."

"How long do you suppose it will take Benedict Howe to catch up with us?" Betty asked.

"Why, I imagine he's lurking around London right now, hoping to catch sight of us, although he can't know I've already discovered his theft of the old paper. I don't believe I mentioned where we were staying in London, so he won't be able to find us to continue pleading his case to visit Paul's father.

"He could be anywhere. Perhaps he's already in Rome. Since he doesn't know what we've uncovered about him, he's probably camped out in a cafe near our hotel, waiting for us to pull up to the door. But don't worry about him. He's a criminal, but I don't think he's dangerous."

"Criminals are always dangerous, especially if they think they're about to be caught. And they have a lot of problems with ethics, it goes without saying. I suppose it's too far-fetched to think he was the one who fired a shot at Mrs. Flood, or perhaps at Mr. Flood, rather than being the target himself."

"But why would he do that? They are paying customers."

"You said that Mrs. Flood has no common sense. Maybe she was importuning Benedict to take her away from the leaky roof, the boring countryside, and her ill-tempered husband, so he decided to rub out Lester. She'd be a wealthy widow, would she not? Or maybe he didn't want to be entangled with Phyllis at all, so he thought he'd dispose of her to get her out of his hair. If a child noticed her 'leaning' on Benedict, other guests at the wedding would have seen the same thing, so suspicion would fall on Lester, the jealous husband. Then Benedict is off to the continent while the authorities try to imagine what took place, and Lester is left holding the bag."

"I'm sure Lester did it," Margaret said, "but what a devious mind you have, Elizabeth."

Betty beamed. "Yes, I do, don't I?"

CHAPTER 8

*T*HE NEXT day found them following the plan Margaret had outlined in the evening. During the time they spent looking at portraits of the royal and the famous at the National Portrait Gallery, Betty half expected to see Benedict Howe sketching/copying/forging a painting. But while there were a number of students earnestly studying the pictures and some were even drawing them, no Benedict was to be found in the quiet rooms they passed through.

Margaret took her to the promised Indian restaurant, where she said her Uncle Lawrence often dined. She presumed that it must be authentic if it met the strict criteria he had developed during his long years in India.

"I'd ring him to ask about Benedict Howe," Margaret said, "but he's terribly old and I don't want to trouble him. He wasn't even strong enough to travel to David's wedding, even though he grew up at the Priory. I think we learned enough about Benedict's relationship with Uncle Lawrence's library from Charles."

"I think," Betty said, "that we know all we need to know about that young man."

They spent the afternoon wandering the streets of London, looking in shop windows. Margaret offered Betty a list of sights to be seen, but Betty decided she'd save her sightseeing for Rome. Finally it was time to make their way to Albemarle Street and Brown's Hotel.

"I've reserved a table for us," Margaret said. "Tea here is very popular." They made their way to the wood-paneled Drawing Room, as the tearoom was called, decorated with antique furnishings. Several people at little tables were already enjoying dainty sandwiches, little cakes, and warm scones with clotted cream and strawberry preserves. Because the day was warm, the big fireplace was not lit, but a pianist played soft tunes in the background.

"Brown's has been around since the early eighteen-hundreds," Margaret said. "It's actually a number of houses joined together, and all sorts of famous people have stayed or lived here. They say Agatha Christie had Brown's in mind when she wrote *At Bertram's Hotel*."

Margaret was pouring a second cup of tea for Betty when someone sank down in the empty third chair at the table.

"Thank goodness I noticed you two sitting here," Phyllis Flood said. "They weren't going to allow me in because I didn't have a reservation. And I'm a guest here," she added indignantly.

"What a surprise," Margaret said. "I didn't know you were planning to come up to London."

"I like to take the train up at least once a week from West Rime," Phyllis said. "One doesn't know how long they'll keep it running because there's not much business nowadays on our line. Everyone prefers to drive rather than take the train. But I point out that you have to do something with your car once you get to the city, and that can be a problem. Parking is *so* difficult and expensive. So I just hop on board and take a taxi here from the station. And once I'm here, I'm close to all the shops I like. Bond Street and Regent Street are just a skip away, and the theater district is close by. I can get to Knightsbridge, too, only two or three stops on the Underground from the Green Park station. And this is a delicious hotel, don't you think? So quiet and re-fined, and you never know who you'll see here. All the best people." Apparently Phyllis did not need to take a breath once she started talking. Margaret in-terrupted the flow of words.

"I assume you're here to consult with Benedict about the painting he's doing for the manor."

"As a matter of fact, I am—and more. Remember I told you that I was thinking of having him do my portrait, and he's agreed to paint me! Won't that be fun, and such a surprise for Lester." Margaret thought there would be even more "surprises" for Lester.

"Benedict is such a charming young man, don't you think? And talented. I spent the morning at his studio looking at his work. Very fine indeed. The work, I mean, not the studio. That's just a dumpy place he borrowed from a friend. But I did want him to get started on my portrait before he went off to Italy. He doesn't know how long he'll be gone, because he has some important business with a dealer, but he took some Polaroids of me so he can think about the picture and make some sketches. He said he might consider doing an Italian landscape as the background. I might even join him there so he can get on with his work. Lester and I had a lovely tour of Italy a few years ago, but it was barely enough time to see everything. Benedict has promised to show me absolutely everything, if I can manage the trip."

Margaret felt compelled to interrupt her again. "Shall I have them bring another cup so you can have some tea?"

"That would be lovely, but no more food. I'm not at all hungry, I'll just have this last little watercress sandwich. I can't stay long, Benedict is picking me up soon and taking me to a friend's for cocktails. The poor dear's shoulder is still a bit painful where the bullet nicked him. I don't understand what possessed Lester. . . . He might have killed him. Anyhow, the friend is a sculptor, and Benedict says he might actually consent to do a marble bust of me, even though it's considered old-fashioned. Don't you just love the bohemian life that artists lead? Miss Trenka, you haven't said a word. Are you finding sightseeing in London tiring? I know that travel can be wearing for an older person. . . ."

Betty resisted the impulse to say that she wasn't quite that old. "I'm finding everything very interesting. It's my first visit."

"I think London is almost more exciting than New York. Benedict says . . ." But they never learned what he said, because he appeared at the door to the Drawing Room wearing a rather grubby white crewneck sweater and paint-spattered trousers. His arm was in a sling. He was gently turned away by the wait staff, who perhaps failed to see the charm of the bohemian lifestyle.

"How insulting," Phyllis said as she watched him back away. "Isn't it obvious that he's an artist? Who do these people think they are?"

"They do recommend smart dress here," Margaret said mildly. "And probably don't make exceptions for artists. I do hope his injury will not hinder his artistic endeavors."

"He's a brave boy," Phyllis said. "He could have been killed by my idiot husband. Lester is an excellent shot. He was probably upset because Ben asked for a substantial advance on the painting he's doing for us. Well, I'll go find the dear boy, and then we're off. So lovely to see you again so soon."

She ducked her head down so she could whisper to the both of them. "You know, Lester got a little upset the other day, but he didn't mean to shoot at Benedict, no matter what those Upper Rime gossips say. He pointed the gun toward the ceiling, just to alarm Benedict, not murder him. Everybody knows Lester wouldn't harm a fly. He just has a problem with his temper, especially these days. He never dreamed that life in the English countryside could be so . . . so . . ."

"Quiet?" Margaret offered.

"Except for overseeing the beastly renovations, he doesn't have much to do. And when Lester is at loose ends, his temper seems to get out of hand."

Phyllis hurried away, and Margaret looked at Betty. "Alarm him? With a random gunshot? I should say."

"And I should say that Mrs. Flood is playing a dangerous game," Betty said. "Do you suppose we shall be treated to Phyllis Flood as an exact copy of the Mona Lisa? Or a newly discovered Da Vinci from the hand of Benedict Howe?"

"Not as far-fetched as it sounds. But I should think it would be someone a little less famous. Now, shall I try to track down some theater tickets for tonight?"

Betty sighed. "I know London theater is very good, Margaret, but I am a bit tired, and we have to be off tomorrow. Would you mind if I begged off?"

"Not at all. All the good plays end up in New York anyhow, so I'll see whatever I miss now on the other side of the Atlantic. I suppose," Margaret added slowly, "that Phyllis must also find country life a bit boring after living in New York. It's not surprising that she's eager to add some excitement to her life when there's a chance."

"As good an excuse as any for tearing after that boy," Betty said. "I hope she doesn't get hurt. I don't mean physically, but emotionally. I don't think bohemians have a handle on treating needy women with great kindness."

"All I can tell you is what Paul told me. That he understood that Benedict preferred men to women."

"Well, what do you know about that?" Betty's experience with homosexual men was extremely limited. There was only that assistant bookkeeper at Edwards & Son who once confessed his sexual preference to her while he was in the throes of a breakup with his partner. He had been a nice, quiet young man, well dressed and good at his job. Betty had never noticed any sign that he was gay, and she'd only became his confidante because he needed a friend in his personal agony and probably didn't think he'd get any comfort or understanding from the flighty clerical girls who were barely out of their teens.

She'd been sympathetic about his plight and had arranged with Sid Senior to have him represent the company at an out-of-state convention. The last they heard, he had found someone new among the exhibitors of hardware products, had resigned from Edwards & Son by letter, and had moved with the new boyfriend to Arizona.

"I'm afraid I don't know much about that sort of thing," Betty said. "It's all a mystery to me."

"Not much to know," Margaret said. "Art, theater, decorating, and those sorts of professions tend to be the ones that attract numbers of gay men. They are as kind or as awful as any other group of people. There's no mystery, except what human beings will get up to. Let's go home before the tube gets too crowded, or we could take a taxi. I'd like that."

Betty decided she would too. She enjoyed the spacious black London taxis.

Margaret called for the bill, and they discovered that Mrs. Flood had taken care of it.

"She can afford it," Margaret said. "I only hope she can afford Benedict Howe. And I don't mean the price he'll charge for his paintings."

Soon they were home at the flat, where Betty spent the evening listening to her conversational Italian tapes and repacking her suitcase for the onward journey.

CHAPTER 9

*B*ETTY TRIED to make mental notes of every step of the way from the flat to Gatwick Airport to report the details to Ted—the train from Victoria Station that took them to the bustling airport, their check-in at the British Airways counter, the wait until boarding, the boarding itself, and the take-off without much delay. Two and a half hours later, as they started to descend toward Fiumicino airport, she could see green fields with little square houses scattered about the countryside, winding dirt roads, a glimpse of a river, a band of highway, and snaking rows of grapevines.

"You missed the Alps," Margaret said. "I'm afraid you dozed off for a minute."

"I'm not especially fond of mountains," Betty said. "I'll see them another time."

Fiumicino proved to be another bustling airport, with a long line at Immigration that moved surprisingly quickly as the official glanced at her passport and stamped it firmly. Then there was another line at Customs after they retrieved their luggage, this one moving slowly so they were delayed despite having nothing to declare. Finally they emerged into the airport waiting area, where Margaret spotted a man holding a sign that said LADDY PRIMA.

"That would be us, I presume," Margaret said. The driver loaded them into a large car, similar to an American sedan but bigger than Betty's Buick back home. As they sped along the highway, Betty caught glimpses of bits of Roman aqueducts marching through the fields. The traffic was heavy, but their driver didn't seem to notice it, and indeed displayed a devil-may-care attitude toward other vehicles.

Once they reached the outskirts of Rome, Betty was delighted to see palm trees in evidence, and plenty of blooming flowers, just like the ones she'd seen in the garden books she'd studied. The city itself was a mass of traffic, with a deafening noise of horns and the occasional vignette of two angry drivers gesturing wildly over some trivial auto-related incident. The accident drew crowds of onlookers who participated in the discussion.

Avoiding the multitude of scooters, many of them ridden by young men talking on cell phones, they moved slowly along impossibly narrow streets where the fronts of the buildings seemed to encroach on the streets. They passed huge domed churches and scooted across piazzas where young people and tourists loitered under shady awnings. Here and there loomed orange and ochre palazzis, and sad clumps of ancient, brown-brick ruins. Elsewhere people sat at little tables in front of cafes sipping wine or espresso. A fruit and vegetable market was just closing down as they passed it, and Betty glimpsed piles of tomatoes, lemons, and oranges that had not been sold or packed up.

There were fountains everywhere, with water tumbling into basins from a lion's head placed on the side of a wall, gushing from the mouth of a fantastical beast, shooting into the air while admired by marble nymphs, gods, and goddesses, or simply spilling from one level to another in little waterfalls.

Finally they drew up to the Hotel D'Inghilterra on the corner of Via Bocca di Leone and Via dei Condotti. Betty noticed the gleaming shops on the nearby streets, and the tourists in shorts and sneakers and the well-dressed local women hurrying by.

"The Spanish Steps are right up that street," Margaret said. "We'll take a stroll there after we're settled, but tomorrow we'll get to some serious sightseeing. We'll make a list tonight—the Trevi Fountain, of course, and Piazza Navona, maybe the market at Campo dei Fiori. I think we'll save the Vatican and St. Peter's for another day."

They stepped into the dimness of the hotel's lobby and walked on black and white marble squares to the desk. Margaret handled their registration and saw to it that their belongings were carried to their room—their suite actually, so they had separate bedrooms. It was as nice as the Villa d'Este in New York, where Carolyn Sue was a part owner and where Betty had stayed during a business trip on Ted Kelso's behalf. The handsome young bellman fussed about showing them the television set, the air-conditioning, the phone, and the lights.

"*Grazie,*" Margaret said.

"*Prego.*" He palmed her tip expertly, and asked in excellent English if the signoras needed anything further.

"Not at the moment," Margaret said, and he bowed as he departed. "He probably thinks I'm a princess or the like. The clerk at the reception desk was especially fawning. 'Lady' does that to people. They all probably think . . ."

". . . we're somebody we're not," Betty finished for her.

"I wonder if I can persuade the hotel to press some of my outfits," Margaret said, as she shook out a pretty mauve silk jacket. "I think I'll wait, and see if hanging my clothes will repair the wrinkles.

"Lunch is the big meal in Italy, and we're too late for that, but we ought to find a little something to welcome you to Rome."

"I would like to get my bearings," Betty said. "That stroll you mentioned . . ."

"Wear comfortable shoes. But we won't venture too far tonight. The Piazza di Spagna is always pretty lively because it's a magnet for tourists and the Roman *ragazzi* looking for pretty American girls to hook up with for a night on the town."

"*Ragazzi* means, if I remember my tapes, simply 'boys.' "

"Correct," Margaret said. "It's used to refer to boys of all ages—little ones, teenagers in packs, any group of free-wheeling young men, I guess."

Suddenly there was a knock on the door. Their bellman had returned, carrying a huge bouquet of roses. "It was left for you, Lady Printom?" He hesitated over her name.

"Priam, yes. Thank you." She opened the little white envelope attached to the roses. "How sweet. Prince Aldo has sent us flowers to welcome us to his city. He invites us to his villa the day after tomorrow for lunch. He will send a car for us at noon. I shouldn't think, from Paul's tales of his father's doubtful financial state, that Prince Aldo could afford a car and driver and a double dose of roses, but Italians do like to show off."

"I suppose," Betty said, "that the next sight we'll see is Benedict Howe, with Phyllis Flood on his arm."

"He wouldn't be foolhardy enough to run off to Rome with Mrs. Flood, or maybe he would. She did say she might decide to make the trip," Margaret said.

"Besides, I imagine Phyllis's preparations for travel to the continent would take quite a bit of time. She's not one to throw a few frocks into an overnight case. She may like the idea of the bohemian life, but I don't believe she's ready to embrace it herself. She requires a lot of support materials to keep her looking youthful and well dressed."

The light was just beginning to fade as they left the hotel and walked slowly toward Piazza di Spagna along Via dei Condotti. Betty peered down the street and there at the end she saw a church and an obelisk atop a hill, and spilling down the hill a broad whitish marble staircase, filled with people sitting on the shallow steps.

The tourists had not yet retreated to their lairs, and the Romans were lounging decoratively on the steps or dashing along the narrow streets on their scooters, creating a tremendous din.

Betty found it curious that lacking a reasonable parking spot, people seemed to park their vehicles on the sidewalks or wherever there was space. When they reached the piazza, she saw flower sellers, ice cream sellers, and a curious boat-shaped fountain sunk into the pavement of the piazza where passersby stopped for a drink of water.

"It's called the Barcaccia," Margaret said. "It's supposed to have the best-tasting water in Rome, according to Paul."

But Betty, instead of looking at the fountain, was gazing with a bemused expression at a McDonald's facing on the piazza. "I guess no place is out of bounds for a golden arch," she said.

"Forget McDonald's. That little house right next to the steps is the house where Keats lived and died. Over there at the back of that space where the cars are parked is the headquarters of Valentino—the designer, not the silent film star. Other designers have showrooms nearby—Niccolo Orsini for one, a favorite of mine. Do you feel up to climbing the steps? I want to take you to a place at the top before sundown."

They looked like easy steps, but Betty was puffing by the time they reached the church at the top, even with stopping to look down at the crowd from the landings.

Margaret gazed up at the church. "It's called Trinità dei Monti. That building is Hassler Villa Medici, a hotel grander than ours. Come along, it's only a short walk."

They walked gradually upward under shady trees as traffic sped down the narrow road. Margaret pointed out the French Academy on their right and told Betty that the Villa Borghese gardens were up ahead. They stopped at a quaint narrow outdoor cafe, draped with vines and a trellis for a roof covered with more vines. It was perched on the side of the hill just off the road.

"This is it," Margaret said. "We'll sit by the railing and have a cool drink and a bite to eat and watch. . . ."

Betty had already found a table by the railing and was watching the setting sun gild the dome of St. Peter's in the distance and highlight the orange, apricot and yellow buildings and roofs below the cafe.

"What a marvelous sight," she murmured. "Thank you."

They settled down with glasses of Prosecco and a plate of panini.

"Champagne and tea sandwiches," Betty said. "A perfect meal."

"The last time I visited Rome," Margaret said, "I came here every morning to drink coffee and read the newspaper."

"Excuse me, are you ladies English?"

The voice behind them jolted Margaret and Betty, who turned as one to see a tall, slim young man with fair hair and merry blue eyes. He was obviously not Italian, even though he wore a handsome green tailored silk shirt and well-cut slacks that fairly screamed Italian fashion. His accent, however, was British.

"Not I," Betty said. "Pure American."

"Yes, I am," Margaret said, somewhat warily.

"I don't mean to interrupt you," the young man said. "I heard you speaking, and I was suddenly homesick for England. My name is Max Grey. I've been living in Rome for several months, and I miss hearing real English that is not laced with an Italian or American accent. My apologies for saying that," he said to Betty.

"Will you join us?" Margaret said. "We've just arrived, and I wanted to show Elizabeth the view to get her into the spirit of the city."

Max pulled over another chair, accepted a glass of Prosecco, and beamed at them expectantly.

"Ah yes . . . I'm Lady Margaret Priam and this is Elizabeth Trenka. Although I'm English, I live in New York, so I understand how it is to miss the sound of home."

Max frowned. "Priam? The people with that big place they call Priam's Priory? The Earl of Brayfield's estate?"

"Why yes. Do you know it? The earl is my brother."

"David's succeeded to the title? I guess I've been

banging around the world so long I didn't know the old earl had passed on."

"Then you know David?"

"Slightly. I suppose you could say that my father and yours were fairly well acquainted, so I was thrown into your brother's company from time to time when we were kids. I guess you were off being finished in Switzerland or some such educational haven for titled young ladies, because I certainly would have remembered you. I haven't seen David for years."

"He was just married," Margaret said. "Elizabeth and I came over from America for the wedding."

"He didn't marry Chloe Waters, did he?"

Margaret shook her head. "No. A local girl. Chloe is a bit too . . . active for David's taste."

"Good show. Chloe is a painful example of young womanhood. I've known her for ages. At one time, her father even viewed me as a perfect mate for her, but I escaped that fate. My father was a bit too snobbish to consider the daughter of a biscuit manufacturer. At the same time, Chloe was convinced that David was her ideal mate. And now he's escaped." Max Grey stood up. "I have an appointment to keep, or I'd stay on to reminisce about Jolly Old. I say, you can usually find me on the Spanish Steps in the afternoon, or someplace nearby like Cafe Greco. Never Babington's, in spite of the English teas they serve. I don't miss England so much that I want to huddle with a room full of tourists, gabbling about the price of things, and bottoms pinched by Italians, and the noise, and the traffic. But now and again I do stop at McDonald's, because sometimes I do want to meet some interesting American tourists, and they flock to the burgers there."

"I trust we'll meet again, Mr. Grey."

"Call me Max, please. Everybody in Rome knows me just as Max. One name, like Madonna or Cher. *Arrivederci*, Signora Trenka, m'lady."

He glided away, pausing to share a laugh with one of the waiters.

"How odd," Margaret said. "My father never mentioned a friend named Grey with a son named Max. And he knows Chloe—well, everybody does—and David as well."

"My father never told me about anyone he knew," Betty said. "He did not share much with his children, only his opinions with which we were not allowed to argue. But it can be a small world, can't it?"

Margaret appeared to be deep in thought. "Wait a moment. I have a vague recollection. . . . Well, never mind, it will come back to me, I'm sure. No, it has. I do remember David talking about his friend Max, but the name wasn't Grey. It was Amber or some such color name. And Daddy had a friend named Augustus Amber who used to come around to the Priory. He must have been Max's father. He was someone in the City who decided to become a country squire. He bred horses and dogs, as I recall, and thought himself very grand. And Max . . . I seem to remember that David told me that Max misbehaved quite badly, but he never told me what he'd done, only that he was sent away, with a stipend as long as he stayed out of England."

"A remittance man, we used to call them," Betty said. "What awful thing did he do that he was banished?"

"No idea," Margaret said. "Perhaps he was too charming for his own good."

"What a pack of scoundrels we have attracted," Betty said. "This is nothing like life in Connecticut."

They finished their wine and strolled back the way they had come. The Spanish Steps were still packed with people, young and old, fashionable and frumpy. Betty gratefully accepted Margaret's suggestion that they sit for a moment to watch the passing parade. Suddenly, Betty nudged Margaret and pointed with her chin toward the Barcaccio fountain.

The vivid green of Max Grey's shirt stood out from the knot of men that surrounded him. Soon Max detached himself and strolled away down Via dei Condotti with an older gray-haired man.

Margaret watched them with narrowed eyes.

"I think I'd like to go back to the hotel," she said. "Plenty of time to become a tourist tomorrow."

CHAPTER 10

BETTY WAS up early the next morning, and when she peeked into Margaret's room, she saw that Margaret was still sleeping soundly. She left her a note, saying she was going out for an hour or two. When she descended to the lobby, she could smell coffee, but she decided to go out in the early light and find coffee at one of the cafes and coffee bars she'd seen yesterday. But first she would return to Piazza di Spagna where she'd noticed the American Express building. She would change some travelers cheques into local money.

She had a few Italian coins that didn't make much sense to her, but she'd examined photos in her guidebook of lira bills in various denominations and hoped she'd figure them out.

Once outside the hotel, she was pleased she had decided to see Rome in the early morning. The traffic never stopped, she decided as she sidestepped a careening motor scooter. Fashionable young shopgirls were scurrying to their jobs at the stores on Via dei Condotti. From above she heard the voices of housewives calling across the narrow streets to their neighbors, and she saw others opening windows in the apartments above the shops, shaking out carpets and pillows on the pedestrians below.

For a time she wandered the narrow streets below the Spanish Steps, and once came upon another small vegetable and fruit market spilling off the pavement onto the street. More housewives were already shopping, carefully picking over the displays and arguing with the market women. She was very proud of herself for successfully navigating the purchase of an orange with as little Italian as possible.

Gradually she made her way to the piazza and into American Express. The Spanish Steps next to the American Express building were already well populated with tourists and locals, everyone seemingly posing, either for photos or simply hoping to be noticed.

The line at the currency exchange window was already several people long, mostly young and casually dressed Americans and Britons, but the line moved quickly, and in a few minutes, she received a wad of lira notes with many zeros on them in exchange for her travelers cheques. She tucked the money away carefully into the deep zippered pocket of her slacks and returned her passport to the zippered case under her shirt. She wore the case on a length of nylon, mindful of the guidebook warnings to protect valuables. The nylon had been proclaimed unbreakable by the salesperson in the luggage shop at the mall near East Moulton where she'd bought it. "Almost impossible to cut, too," he'd said proudly. She felt reasonably secure for the moment.

As she stood near the fountain in the piazza, watching the denizens of the steps mount and descend, she began to feel a little hungry. She knew she could find coffee and food at McDonald's to her right, but it didn't seem proper to begin her first day in Rome at an American fast-food emporium.

"Buon giorno, signora."

Max Grey, looking half-awake around the eyes but as elegantly dressed as the day before, waved to her from the steps, then joined her at the fountain.

"You are an early riser," he said. "Can I offer you a coffee?"

"Good morning . . . er . . . Max. I thought, I'd take a look around before it turned too hot. And yes, I'd love some coffee. I'm not quite sure how the cafes work. . . ."

"If you are able to walk a little distance, I have a sight to show you while we sip our espresso or cappuccino."

Betty shrugged her agreement, and they started off to the right of the piazza, past a tall column around which a few taxis gathered.

"This column commemorates the dogma of the Immaculate Conception of the Virgin Mary and that building is the Collegio di Propagando Fide—propagation of the faith, the Church's ministry of propaganda. Bernini and Borromini both had a hand in creating the façade and the column. Of course they hated each other with a passion. I hope I'm not boring you with religious matters and architecture, but I'm very interested in Rome's architecture."

"Not at all. I was raised in the Church, and I need to learn all I can about the architecture of the city. I'm terribly ignorant."

He led her along streets lined with looming palaces, describing their history. "Don't worry too much about street names, but try to remember landmarks, so you can get back to places you've been."

They entered a square bursting with traffic and people. "This is Piazza San Silvestro. The post office is just over there, if you care to joust with post office workers. Actually, if you're just buying some stamps you should get through without too much confrontation. A lot of buses end their routes here, too, so it's a good place to become familiar with."

They reached a very busy street, and Max waved to someone waiting to cross on the opposite side, "*Ciao*, Mimmo! Be careful, signora. These Italians think of driving as a blood sport. Or bloodless, since they don't often hit anyone, but they like to startle you." They managed to cross what he told her was Via del Tritone, "after a grand fountain up the incline in Piazza Barberini."

Betty heard the swoosh of falling water faintly in the distance. Then a group of Japanese tourists festooned with cameras and led by a brisk young Japanese woman holding a yellow flag passed them. They were all intent on capturing some scenic prey on videotape.

Suddenly they were in a sort of piazza, not too spacious and hemmed in on three sides by shops, a hotel or two, some bars, a church. On the fourth side, against the side of a building, was the Fountain of Trevi, gleaming a brilliant white in the sun. It was an extravagance of marble Neptune and thrashing horses, with cascades of water bouncing and foaming from basin to basin and finally into a large, limpid blue-green pool surrounded by a raised edging of marble on which many people were sitting. Others, including the Japanese party, were snapping photos from every vantage point. A set of shallow steps led from street level to the promenade around the edge of the basin.

"What do you think? Isn't it grand? It's one of my favorite places in Rome," Max said. "A baroque highlight of the city, contrived by someone named Salvi in the seventeen-hundreds. Why don't you have a seat on that wall and drink in the sights while I fetch us some coffee. Cappuccino or espresso?"

Betty couldn't take her eyes off the fountain, but said, "Cappuccino is the one with milk, isn't it? And I'd like a bit of sugar."

"Done," Max said. "Keep your belongings close. The pickpockets hover in the busy tourist areas. And if you see a bunch of quaint, rather dark, and ragged children swarming in your direction, walk briskly up the stairs and into a shop. Do not talk to them or let them get close to you. The gypsies cannot keep their little hands to themselves." Max was off to a cafe before she could mention that one of her close friends at home was an old gypsy woman.

Betty continued to admire the fountain and watch tourists tossing coins over their shoulders into the water. The bottom of the pool was covered with coins, so evidently many, many tourists would be returning to Rome in years to come. Nice reassurance for the tourist industry here, she thought, and looked around. Behind her was a church with grimy walls, and on its steps, of all people, she recognized Benedict Howe leaning against the wall and observing the frantic photographic exploits of the Japanese. He still wore a sling.

She huddled down on her perch so that she was mostly hidden by the balustrade that fenced off the fountain area from the street. She preferred not to encounter Benedict face-to-face without Margaret at her side. Of course, she had the attentive Max . . . but still. And here was Max again, balancing a small coffee cup on top of a larger one, with a plate of small pastries crowning it all.

"They usually won't allow you to take away the cups, but I told Silvio that I was entertaining a very distinguished visitor, a *principessa* perhaps, and he permitted me the luxury of offering you a genuine cup and saucer. He knows that I will return everything. I send all the tourist boys and girls to his cafe when I meet them here at Trevi."

Betty stood and glanced at the church as she sipped the hot, delicious coffee. Benedict had disappeared. She scanned the crowd gathering in front of the fountain but didn't see him anywhere.

"What makes you so interested in Rome's architecture, Max?"

"I studied art history at the university, so it's a good way to put my education to use."

"Not at Oxford, was it?" It would be an alarming coincidence if this smooth operator—he really was very nice and polite—had shared a university education with Benedict Howe, who was somewhere nearby. For all she knew, they could be acquainted. Two slightly shady English boys in Rome—the remittance man and the possible forger—would certainly cross paths. As Margaret had remarked, it wasn't a big city.

Max laughed. "No. I'm afraid by the time I was university age, my reputation had preceded me, and I was not deemed Oxford material. Much to my father's disgust I attended one of the redbrick universities—I mentioned that he's a terrible snob, which is probably why he so enjoyed the company of Lady Margaret's father—then I headed for the sin-and-sun spots of the continent to complete my education on my own. I'm afraid, Miss Trenka, that I am considered a disappointment by my family and even most of my friends."

Just then, a tall older man descended the steps to pool level and walked toward them. To Betty's mild surprise, it was the man with whom she'd seen Max leaving the Spanish Steps the evening before. Margaret's description of Rome as a small city was definitely proving itself correct.

"Ah, Josef, here in good time." Max guided the man toward Betty. "Miss Trenka, may I present my good friend Josef Blum. Josef, Miss Trenka is visiting from America."

Josef Blum rumbled some words in an unidentifiable language, and Max said, "Speak up, old thing," and patted his shoulder affectionately. Blum, wearing a formal suit that complemented his slicked-back gray hair and sharp features, bowed, unsmiling.

"I said," Blum said in a precise, unaccented English, "that Trenka is a Czech name, and one of my dear old friends was a count with the family name of Trenka. I merely asked Miss Trenka if she is a relation."

"Aha! The count! I told you that you were at least a princess." Max seemed pleased with himself.

"No, no," Betty said, flustered. "People often seem to make that mistake, although it is usually an archduke that is mentioned, but I assure you, I am not related to any sort of count or anybody with a title. I am Elizabeth Trenka of East Moulton, Connecticut. That is all."

"Please do not take offense," Blum said. "None was intended. Max, I'm looking for Ben Howe. Have you seen him today? We have some urgent business."

"Didn't know he was back in Rome," Max said.

"I saw him just now over at that church," Betty said without thinking.

The two men looked at her in something close to amazement.

"So you know Ben," Max said. "He certainly gets around, or perhaps you do."

"I met him briefly at a wedding in England," Betty said. "He told me then that he was planning a visit to Rome. I just happened to notice him here today."

"He was looking for me," Josef Blum said. "He can't have gone far."

Eager to get away from them, Betty said, "Max, I think I ought to go back to my hotel. Lady Margaret will be wondering why I've been gone so long, although I did leave her a note. What route should I take?"

"I apologize that I cannot see you to the hotel," Max said. "I have to help Josef track down Ben, but if you walk down that little street to Via del Corso, a very wide, busy street, and turn right, a few streets along you'll find Via dei Condotti. Turn right onto that and you'll reach the hotel. You're staying at the Inghilterra, are you not?"

Betty nodded and wondered how he knew. She didn't recall mentioning it the previous day. "Thank you for the coffee, Max. I hope we'll meet again. Nice to meet you, Mr. Blum. I understand that you were addressing me in Czech, but I assure you, I barely know three words of the language, and those are merely ones my mother used to scold me when I was a child."

Betty departed quickly. It seemed to her that Max and Josef were impatient for her to leave, as though they had confidential matters to discuss. Blum was, admittedly, a handsome older man, but there was something offputting about him.

She found the hotel without difficulty and also found Margaret drinking coffee and eating a cornuto in the breakfast room.

"Well, I'm glad you're back safely. Any adventures?"

"Not really." Then she told Margaret about Max and Benedict and Josef Blum, who thought her related to a count named Trenka. "Even in Rome, I am mistaken for someone I'm not."

"And you are to be found with a pack of strange men gathered around you. You don't waste time. Well, what would you like to see today? You've had your chance at the Trevi Fountain. Let's wander over to the Pantheon and Piazza Navona for more people-watching—and sightseeing."

"I think I know the people we'll watch," Betty said. "They seem to appear whenever I set foot outside."

CHAPTER 11

MARGARET CHECKED the street outside the hotel's door to see if Benedict Howe was lurking in a doorway. "Come along, Elizabeth. Nobody in sight."

They walked briskly down Via dei Condotti to the Corso, where they managed to evade the traffic and reach the opposite side without being damaged. Margaret plunged them into a warren of narrow streets with a few little shops displaying jewelry, electronics, leather handbags, and postcards. Even here in these dark lanes, there were tourists in shorts and T-shirts and comfortable sandals.

Suddenly a sturdy couple up ahead of them was surrounded by a pack of children dressed in long skirts with scarves on their none-too-clean hair, hands outstretched, begging for coins. A few similarly dressed adults huddled in a doorway watching the children beg.

"Gypsies," Margaret said. "You go into that shop there. They won't dare go into a store." Betty obeyed immediately. She didn't like the looks of the grubby children. Meanwhile Margaret sped ahead, just in time to pull one boy's hand from the woman's shoulder bag.

"How nice to see you," Margaret said. "I wanted to show you something in this shop." She grasped an arm of the startled man and woman and steered them into the shop where Betty had taken refuge. The children gathered outside the door and peered in, then slipped away silently.

"I say, what's going on?" the male tourist said. "I'll have the police! Young woman, call the police!"

The shopgirl laughed. "*Signore*, the *signorina* rescue you from the gypsy *bambini*. They are very bad. They want to steal from you. She stop them. The boy is having his hand in the signora's *borsetta*, the handbag, to steal the money. I see him."

"I had to pretend I knew you to make them go away," Margaret said.

"I told you I didn't like the looks of those kids, Harry," the woman said. "And we both read the warnings about the gypsies. Frightening little devils."

"I'm Margaret and this is Betty, and we're on our way to the Pantheon," Margaret said. "If that's where you're headed, we can walk together to fend off further attacks." Harry still looked doubtful.

"What do you say, Edna?"

"I say we're Edna and Harry from Rochester, Minnesota, and they look like perfectly nice ladies to me, Harry. Let's go. I don't want to waste any more time. We've only got this one day left in Rome." Edna marched out the door, followed by

Harry, then Betty and Margaret, who paused to thank the shopgirl for allowing them a haven from the gypsy children.

"They are the curse of these streets on the way to the Pantheon," the shop girl replied. "Sometimes I take the broom to them to sweep them away, but they always come back. *Ciao, signorina.* Come back another day to look at my beautiful jewels."

Margaret promised, and soon the four were on their way, to emerge shortly into a square piazza lined with outdoor cafes. An obelisk and fountain stood in the center, and to their left was the colonnaded and domed Pantheon. Even here, dozens of scooters raced around the piazza or clustered like bees at the edge of the cafes. The tables were filled with tourists and locals admiring the impressive building.

"Harry, I want to look inside right now," Edna said. "Then we can have something to drink." She passed between the columns and into the building. A museum of sorts now, it had once been a church, and before that a Roman temple.

"I'm going to be sitting at a table at that cafe over there," Harry said. "If you run into Edna inside, you can tell her where she'll find me, with a nice little bottle of Italian *birra* in front of me. But you be sure to sit down with us. I want to repay you for rescuing us from those thieving kids." Harry stomped off, and Betty and Margaret entered the Pantheon.

Betty looked around the huge space and then up at the domed ceiling. "My word. All this light is coming in through the hole in the dome." She strolled about admiring the statues and paintings. Little kiosks offered taped descriptions of the building's features in many languages, and there were guidebooks for sale, but neither of the two women wanted an in-depth educational experience.

"Over there," Margaret said, "is where Raphael is buried."

"And right next to Raphael is, if I am not mistaken, Benedict Howe, paying homage to the master. And, my word, I believe that Phyllis Flood is with him."

It was Phyllis, soigné in big dark glasses and a stylish linen suit. They looked a very cozy couple, arm in arm. Benedict had abandoned his sling.

"I don't want to get entangled with either of them at this moment," Margaret said. "Maybe Edna can return the favor and rescue us from an encounter with Benedict. She's right over there."

Margaret tried to accost Edna unobtrusively. "Edna, Harry asked us to find you and then we're all to join him at a cafe outside. He insists on buying Betty and me a drink, and we have another engagement shortly, so we'd like to . . ."

"Harry likes to spoil my fun," Edna said. "He hates culture and foreigners. Oh, I don't mean to insult you two. Anyhow, Betty's not a foreigner. She's American. We do owe you for your help."

"The only thing I ask, Edna, is that we depart as though we're discussing something terribly important. There's someone here we don't want to speak to, so if we're deeply engrossed in conversation, he may hesitate to interrupt." Margaret didn't really think that Benedict would be reluctant to interrupt anything, and she was sure that Phyllis wouldn't pause for a second.

Edna rose to the occasion and began describing the sights she'd seen in Rome with such animated intensity that when Benedict inevitably noticed them, he merely watched the three women leave the building and did not attempt to approach them. Neither did Phyllis, who was determinedly absorbing the artistic and historical atmosphere.

"How did I do?" Edna asked breathlessly as they passed through the doors and between the columns onto the sunny piazza.

"You were perfect," Margaret said. "Ah, there's Harry waving to us. I think I could do with an Orangina or just *acqua con fizz*."

"And *gelato*," Edna said. "I just love Italian ice cream. Harry, you've got to take a look inside. It's magnificent." Edna plopped down heavily on the spindly chair. "And I'm glad you got a table with an umbrella for a change. This Roman sun is a killer."

Margaret noticed Benedict coming out of the Pantheon alone, shading his eyes, but apparently he didn't see her. He walked away from them across the piazza, where he fell into conversation with a group of young men sitting on their immobile scooters admiring passing girls, like cowboys at rest on their horses, keeping watch over the cattle herd.

Near the Pantheon, two *carabinieri* were actually on horseback, their black capes thrown over their shoulders to show the red lining. They too were keeping watch, although the crowd in the piazza was as peaceful as the sea at dawn.

"They have wonderful *tartufo* at that outdoor cafe in Piazza Navona," Edna said as she demolished her ice cream. "Tre Scalini, it's called, because of the three fountains in the piazza."

"I was planning to take Elizabeth there this afternoon," Margaret said. "Not to be missed, the Navona *and* the *tartufo* at Tre Scalini."

"There's so much to see," Betty said.

"So, what was that business about wanting to avoid somebody in the Pantheon?" Edna leaned forward eagerly to get the story.

"It's a young Englishman who is rather following us around," Margaret said. "It's nothing really. He's just tiresome."

Betty nudged Margaret's foot sharply, and Margaret saw that Max Grey had joined Benedict and his Italian friends.

"Two young Englishmen, I meant to say."

"The English are just plain tiresome," Harry said. "If you'll pardon me for saying so, present company excepted and all that."

"It's grand just sitting here," Edna said. "We've been on our feet for hours already. But we got to get moving, Harry. We're supposed to take a look at that church where you stick your hand in this monster's mouth to prove you're telling the truth. If you're not, you get your hand bit off. Remember that movie with Audrey Hepburn? Then we get lunch at the hotel, and I want to have a nap before we do the Rome by Night tour." She turned to Margaret and Betty. "They put you on a bus and take you all around. You see the Colosseum by moonlight, if there is a moon, and you go to nightclubs and see the sights. It's going to be loads of fun, I bet."

Harry stood up wearily. "We'll probably get to see where those damned gypsies sleep and get a look at the hookers. Why, I went out the other night near Piazza di Spagna and the streets were full of them. Holy Rome, you betcha. Okay, Edna, we're on our way. Pleasure to meet you ladies. We probably won't bump into each other again because we're on a bus to Naples in the morning."

"Enjoy the rest of your trip," Margaret said.

"Thanks for the refreshments," Betty said, and they watched Harry and Edna tramp across the piazza before being swallowed up by one of the dark little streets on the other side. Edna, now gypsy-wary, was clutching her handbag against her ample bosom.

"You don't really think Benedict and Max are following us, do you?"

"I doubt it," Margaret said. "It's a small city, and there are certain fashionable places where people congregate."

"Those boys on scooters don't look fashionable to me," Betty said. "Benedict and Max's friends look like old-fashioned American hoodlums. I don't feel like much more walking right now anyhow."

"We don't have to see Piazza Navona today. We can stop there the day after tomorrow."

"I would like to see the Roman Forum some-
time," Betty said. "Way back when I was in high
school, my Latin teacher used to show us pictures of
it, along with making us translate those dreadful
orations of Cicero. I did rather enjoy Latin—it was
different from the Latin used in the Mass—but my
father thought it was a waste of time when I could
have been taking Home Economics."

"We'll have to see the Forum, the Campidoglio,
and the Vittorio Emanuele monument, and the balcony in Palazzo Venezia where Mussolini used to
address the people of Rome. The Colosseum, of
course, and Villa Borghese, and finally St. Peter's
Square and St. Peter's itself. The Sistine Chapel, and
the Vatican Museums, and the apartments with all
the Raphael frescoes. Palazzo Barberini, Piazza del
Popolo. The church of Sant' Ignazio on that dear little piazza. Oh, there's so much to see. We shouldn't
be sitting here, lazing under an umbrella. Navona
isn't far. We can walk there in a few minutes."

They set off, with a backward glance to locate
Benedict and Max. They were still talking, and
Betty thought that Josef Blum had also joined the
group.

"I wonder who Josef Blum is," Betty said. "I find
him a bit sinister."

Margaret stopped and snapped her fingers. "I
think I know. He's an art dealer who has a gallery in
London. He's the one David consulted about some
of the Priory's pictures. He even visited the estate.
Poor David was probably trying to turn up some
cash by selling a picture or two to keep the place

going in the style my father would approve of. No success with Blum, and I'm not sure David would have agreed to sell him anything in the end. I'm surprised that he hasn't rushed up to greet me like an old friend. Max must have told him about meeting me last evening."

They had almost escaped from the piazza when the irritating roar of a scooter was heard behind them. The noise ceased, and Benedict Howe hopped off the back and waved to the driver who departed again quickly.

"I just happened to notice you two," Benedict said. "I knew I'd bump into you in Rome. I know I caught a glimpse of you, Miss Trenka, at the Trevi this morning, having a cozy cuppa with Max. How on earth did you hook up with him? No, never mind. Max has a gift for befriending anything that moves. I hope you're enjoying your visit. I say, Lady Margaret, have you managed to reach Prince Aldo?"

"Ah . . . we have been in contact," Margaret said warily.

"I'm still desperate to get a look at that picture of his. Josef says it's reputed to be a nearly unknown Raphael. I'd give anything . . ."

"So you know Josef Blum? We understood that he was a special friend of Max's."

"Why, yes, Lady Margaret. He keeps Max in line, gets him out of trouble. Josef has a lot of useful connections in Rome, which is fortunate because Max enjoys friendship with a rough crowd when he's not being carried off to an exotic vacation spot by rich old men or women. He boasts that he's killed or nearly killed half a dozen people. All a lie, but he has a vivid fantasy life. I say, Josef claims to have done some business with your family, Lady Margaret. He's an art dealer and has been good to me. He has actually handled a couple of my paintings at his London gallery. He's in Rome now to see what he can pick up. There are still a lot of old pictures around that collectors will grab up if they come from a well-known dealer. You don't find many dealers like Josef willing to take a chance on an unknown like me."

"I believe Mr. Blum was consulted by my brother about a couple of our pictures. That's probably how you knew about the Holbein."

"He did mention it once. Said it was very good, and almost a likeness of your brother. I noticed that after I got a glimpse of it and him at the wedding."

Betty said, "All we're missing here is Phyllis Flood."

"She and I got in yesterday. I just left her in the Pantheon. She wanted to do some shopping. We're staying at the Hassler, at least until Lester comes over in hot pursuit, waving his gun like a gangster. I prefer the Excelsior, but she thinks the Hassler is a better class of hotel. As if she knew anything about class.

"I am greatly in your debt, Lady Margaret. Not only have the Floods commissioned a large landscape, but I'm doing portraits of both of them, possibly in some High Renaissance style so they'll look like ancestral portraits. That's too much of a laugh, if you ask me. Phyllis wants to be dressed in a velvet gown and dripping with antique jewels."

"Then you're still in Lester's good graces, despite his interest in murdering you?"

"It was nothing, Lady Margaret. A misunderstanding. A tiny flare-up of bad temper. A lot of people have wanted to murder me and have failed. I seem to have a gift for getting people's backs up. I'm afraid I have to run off now and do some work. I promised Josef a little picture. I had a good turn of luck and found some paper that's ideal for my work."

"I imagine ideal paper is hard to find," Margaret said. "Especially sixteenth- and seventeenth-century sheets." She and Benedict exchanged a look.

"Sometimes I simply have to seize the opportunity, Lady Margaret. My work is very important to me. But don't forget to plead my case to Prince Aldo. What harm can come from a few glances at a masterpiece? I'll call on you at your hotel one day soon, perhaps even with Phyllis in tow, and we'll have a coffee at Cafe Greco." He signaled to one of his scooter-riding friends, who pocketed his cell phone and hastened to his side. Benedict said something softly in Italian to his friend, jumped on the back of the scooter, and was swept away.

"What presumption! He looked me in the eye and practically admitted to defacing our property, because his work is so very important to him. I like him less and less," Margaret said, "and I certainly will do nothing to persuade Prince Aldo to allow him in to see that picture."

They walked down some short streets and found Piazza Navona, where they admired the three fountains in the oval piazza and the church of St. Agnes in Agony.

"I remember the nuns telling us about St. Agnes," Betty said. "Stripped naked before the people for refusing to marry, but her hair miraculously grew long and covered her nakedness. Then I believe they chopped off her head. She was always held up to us schoolgirls as the model of Christian modesty, representing heaven's assurance that God would protect our virtue, provided we also made an effort to do so." Betty gazed up thoughtfully at the impressive Fountain of the Rivers with its obelisk and massive sculptures representing the rivers of the world. "I used to wonder," Betty said, "why, if she was so virtuous, God allowed her head to be chopped off. But I only asked the nuns once about that because they didn't like the question at all."

CHAPTER 12

BETTY RELUCTANTLY consented to try a *tartufo* at the Tre Scalini outdoor cafe. It seemed to her that Roman days consisted of a constant round of coffees, orange drinks, and ice cream. Still, she was glad she tried the ball of ice cream covered in a shell of chocolate with a plop of sweet whipped cream on top.

"But we didn't have lunch," Margaret said. "The usual two hours of food and then a siesta."

"I'm sure I'd like to try some real Italian spaghetti or pizza—just to see how they compare to the American versions," Betty said. "And there must be all kinds of local dishes that haven't made it to America. I've read that artichokes are a Roman specialty." She turned thoughtful. "I don't actually eat many artichokes back home, but maybe I'll acquire a taste for them here."

"I'm sure Prince Aldo will provide generously tomorrow, and let's hope he suggests we retire for a siesta before we're returned to the city. And I think I forgot to mention that Paul's Italian grandmother is also in residence. Paul describes her as a bit crazy, but I'm sure that like many Italians, he exaggerates. She's probably simply eccentric, the way English aristocrats often are. I remember that Lady Manfred's mother was frequently to be found huddled in a corner of the dining room under a blanket, under the delusion that she was a chicken."

"That's ridiculous," Betty said.

"She was quite certain," Margaret said, "as was her family. I mean, they believed that she believed she was a chicken. She was quite a trial to Lady Manfred, especially when there were to be guests for dinner."

"Ridiculous nonetheless. Chickens don't like a blanket thrown over them. Well, we can handle the old lady. In my time, I've dealt with worse than a chicken delusion. When I was a little girl, Mr. Hough who lived down the street from us was certain that he was a famous singer. Sometimes it was Caruso. He walked the streets of the town all night singing arias at the top of his voice."

"He sounds harmless, if a bit crazed," Margaret said.

"It was not so much the singing," Betty said. "In fact that could be quite delightful on the nights when he thought he was Frank Sinatra. Unfortunately, he had a habit of running after schoolgirls while belting out 'The Song Is You' or 'I'll Never Smile Again.' He was particularly drawn to us parochial schoolgirls in our uniforms. They finally had to put him away after . . ." She stopped.

"After what?"

Betty looked down at the cobblestone ground.

"After he ran after me. He caught me and tried to kiss me. Pop was just coming home from work at the factory and rescued me. But I did kind of miss hearing Mr. Hough sing after he was sent away. In any case, I doubt that the old lady will be any trouble."

"She never liked Carolyn Sue, according to Paul, and is wary of foreign women who might be out to ensnare Prince Aldo the way Carolyn Sue did."

Betty laughed. "I think she should have no worries about me in that regard. But you are a different story—young, blond, and pretty. . . ."

"But not in the market for an Italian prince. I think you would have to be very young and impressionable to fancy one. Carolyn Sue was practically a baby when she fell for him. I say, let's have a look at some of the shops around the piazza, then we'll stroll over to see the Wedding Cake and the Colosseum in the distance, then home. I think I've almost walked enough today, but I don't want you to miss anything."

So they walked some more, and Betty bought some souvenirs to bring home to friends. Margaret showed her Sant' Ignazio, a grand church dedicated to St. Francis Xavier, with masses of baroque decorations and trompe l'oeil paintings. The little square on which the church stood seemed almost perfect with neat burnt sienna palazzi around the edges, and very quiet compared to the rest of Rome. A little further on, they stepped onto the pavement of Via del Corso and, looking right, saw the huge white Vittorio Emanuele monument at the end of Piazza Venezia.

"I know where I am," Betty said proudly. "If we cross over and walk to the left, we'll get to Via dei Condotti and then the hotel."

"Let's walk on this side of the street," Margaret said. "We can catch a glimpse of the garden of the Doria Palazzo, then we'll cross the Corso and stop at Galleria Colonna. There are chairs there if I remember correctly, although it will probably require one more cup of espresso if we want to linger for a few minutes."

Sitting down was good, Betty decided. She bought some postcards to write to Ted and some of her old friends in Hartford, to Molly Perkins, the wife of East Moulton's pharmacist, to the librarian at the town library where she volunteered, and to the teachers at the East Moulton school where she'd been the temporary secretary.

She couldn't forget Penny Saks, her near neighbor on Timberhill Road, plus cards for Penny's three boys, Whitey One, Two, and Three, so called because they were nearly interchangeable blonds. Tina the cat would have to do without a card. With any luck, Tina would be happily living in the Saks household rather than at Betty's house, possibly finding true happiness tripping over Penny Saks's glue guns and paintbrushes. Penny's devotion to crafts was legendary along Timberhill Road. Few neighbors were without an object she had decorated with gilded macaroni.

Margaret wrote only two cards, one of which, Betty noted surreptitiously, was addressed to Sam De Vere. Betty remembered meeting him in New York with Prince Paul, and understood that he was Margaret's serious romantic interest. The other was to Poppy Dill, a widely read New York society gossip columnist.

"Max Grey showed me where the post office is. It's not far from here," Betty said.

"I think I'm not up to dealing with Roman bureaucracy. They'll have stamps at the hotel."

It was a relief to return to the hotel, put their weary feet up, and read for a time as the day faded and the blue Roman sky, flecked with pinkish clouds, turned pale.

"At least it wasn't stiflingly hot today," Margaret said, "although Edna was right about the sun here being a killer. But it was warm enough and will probably be hotter tomorrow. I suppose Prince Aldo's Villa Carolina up in the Alban Hills will be much cooler than the city. After all, that's why the popes and cardinals and the nobility built their villas there—to escape the heat. I think I will have a bath now and wash off the grime. Then I'll decide what to wear tomorrow."

"I don't have all that much to choose from," Betty said. "I don't need be too formal, do I?"

"It's a bucolic estate. I imagine casual dress is perfectly acceptable. Comfortable shoes, as always. Be prepared to tramp through some more gardens. I remember Paul telling me that the water garden is his father's pride and joy."

"As long as I don't have to discuss with an expert the merits of mulching," Betty said, "I enjoy a nice garden. Ted Kelso has a beautiful garden that he tends to himself, in spite of being mostly confined to a wheelchair, although he does have help for the heavy work. He now has hopes of being cured. I can't imagine what it would be like to be helpless. . . ."

The telephone interrupted her.

"Who could that be? I hope there's no trouble at the Priory." Margaret picked up the receiver. "*Pronto*. Ah, yes, she's right here." Margaret handed the phone to a puzzled Betty. "Josef Blum," she whispered.

"For me?" Betty put the receiver to her ear. "Elizabeth Trenka." Then she listened for a time. "Well, thank you. I . . . I'll have to check with Lady Margaret; she may have made plans." She covered the receiver with her hand so Blum couldn't hear her.

Margaret leaned forward expectantly.

"Mr. Blum is inviting me to dine tonight. I don't know the man, just met him in passing. What should I say?"

"Whatever you are comfortable with." Margaret frowned. "I suspect he wants to pressure you about getting Prince Aldo to allow Benedict to see that painting of his. But I'm sure he'll treat you to a nice meal. And I don't imagine he has designs on you, so you won't have to call on St. Agnes to protect your virtue. Besides, I think he might be referred to as an old queen of the old school."

Betty almost giggled. "I believe you must be right

about the painting. It might be fun to go out to dinner with him and find out what he's up to." She uncovered the speaker, and said, "As it happens, I am free tonight, Mr. Blum. Lady Margaret has another engagement. You'll come to the hotel at eight? I look forward to it."

"I'm sure it will be interesting," Margaret said. "But don't make him any promises."

"Certainly not," Betty said. "Besides, I don't know the prince and don't have any influence over him. Oh, dear. It's the what-to-wear problem again."

"Mr. Blum seems a suave continental sort, probably an habitué of the finest restaurants Rome has to offer. You may get that authentic local food sooner than expected. I suggest something more than merely casual."

Betty winced. "I have a sort of basic black dress with one of those chiffon jackets in a flower print. In case I end up somewhere with fierce air-conditioning."

"Probably not in Rome, but it sounds fine."

"What will you do this evening, Margaret?"

"Perhaps a stroll in the area, or a drink in the bar. I don't much feel like a stab at Roman nightlife. I might end up in a reunion with Edna and Harry in the course of their Rome by Night tour."

"I can't say that I'm prepared myself for hot times in Rome," Betty said, "but let's see what Mr. Blum has in mind."

CHAPTER 13

M ARGARET SUGGESTED that Betty remain in the suite until the desk rang her to announce Josef Blum's arrival, rather than waiting in the lobby for him. He arrived promptly at eight.

"Not a typically Roman thing to do," Margaret said, "appearing on time, but of course, he's not Italian. More likely German. Shall I go down with you?"

"If you'd like. He might be Czech, since he addressed me in that language when he thought I was a relic of the Austro-Hungarian Empire. If you're with me, at least he'll know that someone knows where I've gone, if he takes it into his head to kidnap me."

"He doesn't seem the type. You look very nice, Elizabeth, whereas I look wrinkled and touristy, so I don't believe he'll feel compelled to invite me to join you. Not seriously anyhow. He'll probably tender a pro forma invitation, which I will of course refuse with some excuse."

Josef Blum, elegantly tailored, awaited Betty near the reception desk. "Good evening, Miss Trenka.

I'm delighted you could join me on such short notice. And Lady Margaret! May I invite you to join us?" The insincerity of the invitation caused Betty and Margaret to exchange glances.

"How kind, but I'm afraid I've caught a chill. I'd prefer to have a drink at the bar and then go off to bed. I don't want to waste my few days in Rome with illness."

"Please do convey my regards to Prince Aldo when you see him." With that, Blum swept Betty away, out of the hotel, and onto the street, where an amazing low, sleek sports car in brilliant red sat at the door, guarded by a dark-eyed boy, a child really. Blum handed the boy a handful of lire and opened the car door for Betty.

"You must be thinking that this car is a bit sportif for an old gentleman such as myself. It actually belongs to Max, but he has allowed me to borrow it for the evening. I hope you do not find my driving too distressing. Even after years of driving in Rome, I have not mastered all the fearless driving techniques that Romans seem to be born with." He smiled, and Betty found it slightly sinister. "But I shall return you safely. Self-preservation is one instinct I cultivate assiduously. Excuse me for a moment." Blum dialed a number on his cell phone, spoke quickly and inaudibly to the person who answered, and then tucked the phone away.

They pulled away from the hotel and the car's engine hummed with assurance. The streets were dim, and as they skirted the Piazza di Spagna, Betty saw that the Spanish Steps continued to bustle with people. She remembered a famous photograph of her old friend Violetta, the legendary fashion model who had been Tina's original owner, floating down those same steps in a spectacular gown with the skirt billowing in the breeze. A very small world indeed.

"In lieu of a formal dinner, I have arranged for us to attend a small gathering of friends," Josef said. "They have a lovely home just outside the city. Cocktails and a little food. I hope you find them interesting. They always attract the artistic and literary community here in Rome. I'm sure you'll find it most entertaining."

Oh dear, Betty thought, I'll have to pretend to be artistic or literary or both.

Blum proceeded cautiously along narrow darkened streets illuminated only by occasional lamps high on the sides of the buildings. Betty caught glimpses of women standing in shadowy doorways in tight, seductive dresses, their dark eyes following their progress. Harry's Roman hookers, no doubt. Some called out as the car passed, and she thought they were calling to "Maxie." Apparently Max Grey had friends at all levels of society. His car was certainly well known to the ladies of the night.

Blum confirmed it. "Dear Max makes friends wherever he goes. The girls treat him like a pet, and he does chauffeur them around the city on their business or his. I just wish he didn't have that penchant for getting into trouble and taking up with doubtful friends. He does not hesitate to defend what he deems to be his rights. Nor is he subtle. He has learned bad habits from the low creatures he knows, although some of those creatures are quite fetching."

They swept past some lighted fountains where the spray sparkled as it rose and fell back. Soon they were on a dark road lined with squat pine trees. Every now and then, Betty caught sight of tumbled ruins like skeletons of the Roman Empire.

"This is Via Appia Antica," Blum said, "and up ahead is the tomb of Celia Metella, a very famous sight. She was not a terribly interesting person; only her tomb is of interest. We're riding on a road where the Roman legions marched centuries ago, and this is now a very fashionable neighborhood. Our host and hostess are also very fashionable and successful. He is a film director who still manages to find a good deal of work, even though the golden age of Cinecitta and Italian film spectaculars has faded from what it was in the fifties and sixties. Ah, those were the days. I remember when Elizabeth Taylor and Richard Burton turned the city upside down when they were filming *Cleopatra*. Via Veneto was the center of the world then, and the cafes on the pavements of the Veneto were crammed with the Beautiful People. There was a delightful club called Pipistrello—the Bat—where we used to go to listen to a wonderful piano player. I sometimes tease Max that he was born too late to experience *la dolce vita* in its purest form. He tells me that *la vita* may not be as *dolce* now, but he prefers sour to sweetness, so the present suits him quite well."

"And what of Benedict Howe?" Betty asked almost without thinking. "What does he prefer?"

"Benedict is a first-class scoundrel," Blum said. "He has no real preferences other than himself, although he must see something in that dreadful Flood woman that I have missed. She implies that she sees herself as a patroness of the arts, so she may well be of use to him. And to me, as she hints she might use my services to acquire artworks for her home in England.

"Ben is charming, of course, and extremely talented, but he does not yet fully understand where his true talent lies. It is not in his own person, but in his ability to be recognized as someone else." Betty understood that quite well. "I think Ben enjoys too much living life on the edge, balancing himself on a tightrope over a rushing river. Here we are."

Blum turned into a long, winding drive that brought them to a modest house nearly invisible behind a high, thick hedge beyond which she could see a row of slim cypress trees. Several cars were parked outside the hedge, all of them as sleek and expensive-looking as Max's red auto. Betty could hear music coming from the house, but thankfully it was popular tunes rather than the classical music that the artistic and literary establishment might choose as background for a cocktail hour in the Roman countryside.

She hoped only that someone spoke English, as her Italian tapes had taught her little more than a polite *please* and *thank you*. She didn't think the sort of people likely to be in attendance this evening would enjoy the pantomimed verbs that Ted had suggested.

Behind the hedge, tables and chairs were scattered about a lawn, and torches flamed around the perimeter, casting light on languid figures holding glasses and sampling hors d'oeuvres and pastries from a long buffet table. A low amber-colored house with an orange tile roof was almost hidden behind a protective barrier of bright magenta, purple, and red bougainvillea bushes. Betty's cold feet at the sight of all this were very cold indeed, for it seemed that the group was of unimaginably elegant and assured old friends together to enjoy the warm evening, and nowhere did she hear the sound of English being spoken. Her little black dress must be totally inadequate in the midst of what appeared to be the height of fashion, in spite of the few tasteful pieces of Sid's jewelry she'd brought along on the trip.

As they hesitated at the opening in the hedge, an extremely beautiful dark-haired woman in clinging white broke from the crowd and approached them. "*Ciao*, Josef!" Josef walked toward her, took her hand, and kissed it gallantly.

Betty knew that she recognized her as someone famous, but who? She came up with the name. It was Mirella Albani, of course. A legendary film actress who had conquered America a number of years ago in lavish Italian-made Technicolor extravaganzas, and then she'd conquered Hollywood as an unexpectedly sensitive dramatic actress. She seemed not to have aged much in the forty years she'd been a star. Even Betty, who didn't spend much time at the movies, knew who Mirella was, thanks to late-night showings of her films on television.

Betty hung back until Blum motioned her to join them. "Ella, here is Miss Elizabeth Trenka from America. Miss Trenka, our hostess, Mirella Albani."

"How good of you to join us," Mirella said. "Josef always knows the most delightful people."

Betty, who did not feel especially delightful at the moment, was relieved to hear her perfect English.

"How do you do?" Betty said. "I've long admired your films." Polite lie. She had no particular fondness for any of Mirella's films.

"It is kind of you to say so," the actress said. "Josef, Piero is somewhere among that crowd. I know he wishes to see you. I will introduce Miss . . . Trenka to some of our guests."

Josef actually patted Betty's hand in a protective way. "I won't abandon you, my dear, and I am sure Ella will find you a comfortable seat and some interesting companions." He drifted away to seek out Piero, whoever he might be. Ah, yes, Mirella's husband. This was far too elevated an event for Betty's tastes.

"My husband is a great collector of art," Mirella said, "and Josef has been so helpful in building his collection. I will show it to you later if you desire. Now, would you care for something to drink? Angelo, Prosecco! *Subito!*" A white-jacketed waiter rushed to provide Betty with a glass containing the pale wine that throbbed with bubbles. "I think you will be comfortable at that little table near the house, and I will bring some charming people to meet you. Have you an interest in art or music? Literature? Or religion perhaps? The cardinal arrived just a short time ago, such a wise man. Ah, here is Niccolo Orsini. Perfect. He is a wonderful gossip." Mirella linked arms with a tall, well-built, and very tanned man and guided him and Betty to the table.

"Nico, this is Elizabeth, an American visitor and a friend of Josef's. Elizabeth, Niccolo is a fashion designer of whom you must have heard."

"Why, yes, of course." She had, and Margaret had proclaimed him one of her personal favorites, but Betty had never considered donning any of his high-priced garments, which were far too youthful for her in any case.

"Nico, have a little chat with Elizabeth and tell her who all these people are, but if you must leave her, be sure to find her a companion. I must circulate." She used an Italian word, but Betty understood that she needed to attend to her other guests.

"Signora, I will be happy to tell you who these people are, as Mirella has instructed, but I wonder if their names will mean much to you."

"I am interested in people," Betty said. "And I know that gossip is the lifeblood of society, but I never repeat what I hear."

"Excellent. That boy with the beautiful muscles and the disgraceful athletic shoes is one of our most famous footballers. I believe you know it as soccer in America. You do not need to meet him. He has no conversation, but he is much pursued for his ... athletic equipment. The fat gentleman fawning over him is a politico who is rumored to be owned by the Mafia. And those thugs beside him are his bodyguards. They are true mafiosi, not like the pale imitations that you celebrate in America. Old Roberto is not a bad man, and can do great favors for his friends. It is the Italian way. I will introduce you, but I do not think you will need favors from him. Anna, Lelia, *vieni qua*."

Two painfully thin but still sultry young women glided toward Niccolo. He introduced them to Betty as two of his favorite fashion models. It turned out that they also did not have much conversation, and what there was of it was in accented English. The one called Lelia said petulantly, "Nico, *caro*, *il marchese* is begging to take me away now. He says if I do not come with him, he will wait for Max Grey and take him off to Marrakech for a holiday."

"The *marchese*, Signora Elizabeth, is that older gentleman with the red rose in his buttonhole. No sense of style at all. He does not care who he takes away as long as he or she is reasonably handsome. Leila, *carissima*, don't become involved with him, I beg you. He does not have as much money as he boasts. I know this. If he wishes to lavish what he has on a trollop like Max, that is his concern. Trust Nico on this. He will only ruin your face and your figure. Run along, girls. You have fittings in the morning."

"I wonder," Betty said, "if the Max Grey you

mentioned is the same Max Grey I know. A rather tall, good-looking, and blond young man. English by birth. I gather that he has a certain notoriety in Rome."

Niccolo looked briefly taken aback. "I think there cannot be two notorious Max Greys of that description in Rome. And now you have made me curious. How does a distinguished American lady visitor know a person such as Max Grey? Ah, I see. You came here with Josef, so that is answered. They are a team in many ways. But I might ask how you know Josef. Are you a collector or even an artist?"

"Neither," Betty said. "I met Max by chance when I first arrived in the city. He introduced me to Josef, who, for reasons not clear to me, invited me to accompany him this evening."

"You can be certain there are reasons, even if they are obscure at this time. Josef does nothing without a purpose." At that moment, Josef Blum was deep in conversation with a large florid man in a white suit. "He is even now convincing Piero Pannini, the director and the husband of Mirella, to purchase some very expensive but possibly unauthenticated work of art. Piero is, as the Americans say it, a sucker."

Niccolo shrugged generously. "But it is Piero's money to waste, and better to waste it on a pretty picture than hand it over to the Italian tax authorities." He looked at Betty seriously. "I hope, signora, that you do not become too entangled with either Max Grey or Josef Blum."

"I do not intend to," she said. "I am visiting

Rome with a friend, Lady Margaret Priam, from England. We have only a few days here, so I don't think there will be much opportunity to become entangled. When Josef asked me to accompany him tonight, I accepted because I was curious to learn why he selected me. I am not an art collector with money or much of anything else to recommend me. I think perhaps he wants to befriend me because tomorrow I am visiting Prince Aldo Castrocani, who is . . ."

"I know who he is," Niccolo said cheerfully. "When I was starting out in the couture business, the lovely Carolina, his wife at the time, was one of my first clients. Her American dollars and her recommendations made my career possible. I have long hoped that Aldo would find another wife who was as acquisitive as Carolina. But why would Josef need to use you to reach Aldo? Ah, I have it! The Raphael that he supposedly owns and refuses to show to anyone. And you are an intimate of *il principe*, perhaps even a relative. Josef would like to get his hands on it."

"Does everyone know everything about everybody here?" Betty asked, not bothering to deny that she was related to anyone in Rome.

"*I* know everything about everyone," the designer said. "It is quite a small city. And now I know about you, *principessa*."

"No, no," Betty said. "The only princess I know is your friend Carolyn Sue, but I may meet Prince Aldo's mother when I visit his villa with Lady Margaret." She had that sinking feeling that came over her when she was mistaken for someone she was not.

Niccolo tossed back his head and laughed. "About her everyone knows. She was a heroine during the war, and they say she killed a dozen German soldiers by her hand alone. The Germans retaliated by killing a dozen or more Italians—children, young men, old men—including her husband the prince, leaving Aldo, barely more than a baby, to inherit the title. After that her mind failed her and she was sent to Switzerland to recover it. She did not—she is still *pazza*—but is now under the care of Aldo.

"Ah, look, there is Giancarlo, our most famous pop star, in serious conversation with one of our most famous writers, Anna Peretti. I wonder what they could have to talk about. He is a peasant of limited talent and education, and she is a remarkably dull woman who is capable of producing many dull words on paper."

The gossip had not yet begun to interest Betty, and she wondered how she could politely detach herself from Orsini. In her career at Edwards & Son, she had often managed to halt tedious or unwanted conversations by suddenly inquiring after the speaker's health, about which, logically, she should know nothing. So she suddenly said, "Mr. Orsini, have you had that eye problem taken care of? It can turn serious, you know."

Niccolo looked at her blankly for a moment.

"At the moment, I can clearly see his eminence the cardinal, and I do want to speak to him before he leaves. If you'll excuse me, signora." The de-

signer fled in the direction of a distinguished gentleman in a clerical collar, with a touch of red against
his black garments. Betty smiled to herself. Now
what to do for companionship? She didn't care to
speak to Josef Blum, who seemed to have disappeared, in any case. The well-coiffed and smartly
dressed Roman matrons sprinkled through the
crowd, with their proud noses and disdainful looks,
were not likely to welcome her, nor would Niccolo
Orsini's models or the national pop and sports stars.

Just then she was delighted and surprised to see
Margaret's blond head among the masses of drinking, eating, and chatting guests, but as she got to her
feet, she discovered that Margaret had Benedict
Howe in tow, along with Phyllis and Lester Flood.
Then she saw that Niccolo had cornered Max Grey
and was perhaps urging him to depart for Marrakech with the *marchese* so as to keep his models
safely in Rome.

Soon Ben and Josef joined Max, and Niccolo detached himself. Then Betty observed what could
only be an argument involving the art dealer and the
two young men.

Since none of them was Italian, the eloquent hand
gestures that she'd noticed were natural to Italians
in her tour of the city were not evident here, but
some sort of conflict was definitely occurring. Eventually, even Phyllis and Lester were observing the
trio with interest.

My word, Betty thought, every person I know in
Rome is here. And she had a feeling that this was
not a good omen.

Margaret made her way to Betty's side.

"All the people I'd rather not meet at a cocktail party are here tonight," Margaret said. "But I've found someone who will return us to the city at once. Are you ready to leave?"

"Need you ask?" Betty said.

CHAPTER 14

"*THE FLOODS,* Benedict, Max, and I came by hired car," Margaret said, "and Benedict told me I could use it if I wanted to leave early for the city, as long as the driver was told to return for the rest of them. It's all paid for by the Floods, incidentally. I do hope everyone behaves, because Mirella is a nice woman, and I'd hate to have her party disrupted."

"How so?"

"Well, Lester appeared at the Hassler unexpectedly and continues to be in a silent rage over Phyllis flying off to Rome with Benedict. The 'Italian background for my portrait' excuse is pretty thin. I became involved when Max appeared at the Inghilterra saying Josef had summoned him to this place and he was to bring me. He said you needed me. Do you?"

"Not in the least, although I'm glad to see you. I've been treated to an ocean of local gossip by that fashion designer you mentioned, Niccolo Orsini, who puts Molly Perkins, my East Moulton gossip, to shame. . . ."

"I *love* Orsini's clothes. Just my style."

145

"We're such chums now that I'm sure I could arrange to get you into his atelier for a private viewing of his collection, provided I promise not to attempt to wear his clothes. Just why did Josef want Max to bring you here?"

"It was as we expected. To persuade me or us to pressure Prince Aldo into showing Benedict the picture."

"Niccolo seemed to suggest that Josef wants it so that he can sell it to Piero Pannini."

"And Benedict says he just wants to see it. His attitude made me a bit nervous. Menacing in a way, as though nothing was going to prevent him from doing so. He said it was his 'right' to see it. Ah, here's our car." Then she whispered to Betty, "No discussion of Phyllis, Lester, and the others. I don't know how well the driver understands English, and I wouldn't want him to share our views with them."

So instead of talking about the Max-Benedict-Flood group, Betty told her what Niccolo had said about the wartime experience of Paul's grandmother.

"There was another similar incident that was memorialized right out here on Via Appia," Margaret said. "The partisans killed thirty or so Germans, and the Germans retaliated by shooting ten times that many Italian men and boys—even priests—and burying them out here in a pit near the catacombs. The Romans recovered the bodies and created Fosse Ardeatine as a memorial."

"But the old princess didn't get a memorial for her dead," Betty said. "She just had the villa to recall the good old days, and then her son brought in a rich interloper from Texas who wanted to change things. I suppose that's why her mind failed."

The driver was a true son of Rome behind the wheel. He careened into the city and made a circuit around Piazza Venezia and the Vittorio Emanuele monument, giving Betty a glimpse of the Colosseum lit up for the pleasure of Harry and Edna and their Rome by Night tour.

After they reached the hotel, Margaret instructed the driver to return to Mirella and Piero's home to await the Floods and their party. As soon as they were alone, Margaret described in detail how she had joined the party.

"I was sitting at the bar when Max and Benedict appeared, insisting that I join the jaunt to Via Appia and incidentally come to your aid. They made a great fuss about how much you needed me, which was a worry, so I agreed to join them. I can't imagine how they knew where to find me."

"Well, you did mention that you might go for a stroll or have a drink at the hotel bar, and he probably informed Max or somebody. Anyhow, as soon as we got into the car, he called someone on his cell phone—Max or Benedict, probably. Of course I didn't understand a word he said, but that must have been how they knew where you were, and they hurried right to the hotel."

"When we picked up Phyllis and Lester, she implied that Mirella and Piero were dear old friends who had invited her to cocktails, but I'm certain that's not true. The invitation was for Max and

Benedict by way of Josef. . . . Ben simply wanted to take Phyllis along to further agitate Lester."

"Josef is Piero's art adviser. . . ." Betty said. "So you think Phyllis lied."

"I base my belief that Phyllis lied about knowing Mirella on the fact that when she encountered her, the brightest star in the film firmament had no idea who Phyllis was and asked if perhaps she had come to the wrong house. Phyllis had the decency to blush, while Lester was merely red with rage at being dragged out to the Campagna by Benedict. At least Lester didn't try to throttle him then and there."

"I mentioned that I had quite a chat with Niccolo. He did not have kind things to say about Max Grey, and he told me that Josef probably wants to get his hands on Prince Aldo's Raphael in order to sell it to Piero. Do you suppose he intends to steal it?"

"He can't if Aldo won't let him in the door," Margaret said. "Well, we'll warn Aldo about them all tomorrow." Margaret stretched out her arms and yawned. "I need my bed. What a bunch of characters we've hooked up with."

"The day will be hot," Margaret told Betty the next morning as they strolled out to drink a cappuccino. It wasn't hot yet, but the shimmering haze over the city told the tale. The tourist buses were out in force, hurtling their passengers toward the first monument viewing of the day. "We need to be ready by noon, but let's go to the Campidoglio and have a look down at the Forum before it's flooded with tourists. I remember coming to Rome years ago and wandering freely around the ruins, not having to pay a lira for the privilege."

They walked down the Corso and crossed Piazza Venezia at some peril from the swirling traffic, but they joined a Japanese tourist group and found safety in their numbers as the flag-wielding guide managed to persuade the careening autos to avoid them. The Japanese paused in front of the Vittorio Emanuele monument for photos, but Betty and Margaret proceeded onward to the nearby shallow flight of steps and ascended to Michelangelo's beautiful square at the top of the Capitoline Hill.

Margaret paused at the spot where the bronze statue of Marcus Aurelius on horseback had formerly stood. Then she motioned to Betty to follow her between the museums that lined the square to the far side of the Campidoglio. They stood at a railing where they could look down on the Forum, the triumphal arches, and the few remaining columns where temples had once stood.

"I'd like to come back and walk around," Betty said. "There seem to be quite a few cats lounging among the ruins here. I've seen them everywhere. Much as I hate to admit it, I rather miss the awful creature who believes herself to be my cat and my responsibility."

"These are a mere handful of the cats that inhabit Rome," Margaret said. "At Largo Argentina there are hundreds and hundreds of them. Old ladies bring them leftover spaghetti, which the cats love, and there's even an organization devoted to their care. We'll find time to visit the cat city, and to come here again. Now we should be returning to the hotel to get ready for the prince."

Back at the hotel, they quickly changed clothes— Margaret into a yellow short-sleeved dress with a full skirt, and Betty into the sturdy khaki skirt and cotton plaid shirt that Margaret deemed suitable for a visit to the country. They were ready when the car sent by Prince Aldo arrived at noon. It was a roomy silver Fiat sedan with intense air-conditioning against the predicted sweltering heat of the day. Part of the trip took them along the Via Appia, which Betty now saw in daylight, and she admired Roman pines and cypresses along the road and the glimpses of flower-decked villas behind hedges. The tourist buses were plentiful here, too, disgorging visitors along the road at the several catacombs. Soon, however, the car began to climb as they approached the Alban hills. Betty viewed with interest the flat Roman Campagna they were leaving, and looking back, she caught glimpses of the city and the dome of St. Peter's. The way to Villa Carolina took them through prosperous suburbs with comfortable houses.

"What a pleasant place to live," Betty said. "Probably a lot quieter than the city itself."

The car turned off the main road onto a narrower winding street, with the houses farther apart. Some of these impressive villas, their driver told them in careful English, had once belonged to *cardinale*, *il papa*, and the nobility. Now they were either museums for the rich tourists or the property of great old families and the newly wealthy who wanted a traditional country retreat.

"Disgraziata," he said. "What of the poor? The working classes? Do they share in this bounty?" Then he confessed that he was a communist.

"I don't believe that I've ever associated with a communist," Betty said. "Although there was that dedicated Socialist and his wife who were neighbors of mine many years ago. They invited me to a Socialist picnic somewhere in the country near Waterbury. When I asked if I could bring anything, they said no. But when the picnic was under way, all these Socialists never thought to share the beer and soda they'd brought, although they did harangue an innocent young woman, a chance invitee like me, about persuading her father to donate his house 'to the people.' Property was apparently more worth sharing than a Coca-Cola or a Budweiser. It was a very tiresome afternoon, but I did shake the hand of a legendary and perpetual political candidate who ran for ages on the Socialist ticket." Betty smiled. "Alas, no beer, no vote." Betty tapped the driver on the shoulder. "If you are a communist, why do you work for an aristocrat?"

"Eh, Aldo is a good fellow, good to the people who work on his estate. When the revolution comes, we find a place for him. Besides, he knows film stars, television stars, sports stars."

"Well, I know them too," Betty said.

"Signora, I bow to you." He turned slightly to look at Betty in the course of negotiating a curve so the car swerved dangerously.

In a few minutes, they were passing through a tiny village of old houses and across a town square with a shabby fountain in the center. The houses had blue or green shutters closed against the sun and strings of laundry hanging outside. They passed a church and two cafes on opposite sides of the town square, the tables of each filled with grizzled old men. There was a *salumeria* with fat salamis hanging in the window, and a bakery from which an elderly woman in black with snow-white hair emerged with a basket holding two long loaves on her arm.

"The village is called Ingranno," the driver said. "It means trick, a deceit. The people here are old-fashioned and full of trickery. The old lady there is Principessa Olympia herself, Aldo's mother. She walks to the village every day to buy the bread, even though she has servants to do this. She is not right in the head, but people respect her because of what she did during the war."

The old woman was trudging up the narrow main street under the drying laundry. Housewives called greetings to her from the apartments above the shops.

"Should we offer her a ride to the villa?"

The driver shrugged. "She would only refuse. She believes that walking has kept her alive for so long. She is strong and stubborn, and as full of tricks as the village. *Ecco!*"

They had reached the top of the hill where a narrow park on the hillside played host to children, young lovers, and old men on benches. Below the park the Roman Campagna stretched out toward Rome, with the ever-present dome of St. Peter's rising above the city. The hillsides were covered with rows of grapevines, with the occasional old silvery olive tree. They had left Principessa Olympia far behind.

"Margaret," Betty said urgently. "Can that be Benedict and Max in the park?"

Margaret peered out the car's window. "They or people very like them. I don't care for this. It's like being followed." In the little parking area on the edge of the park sat the shiny red car in which Josef Blum had carried Betty off the night before. It was Max's car. This time, Margaret and Betty hadn't been followed but preceded again.

At the very crest of the hill above the park and road, a huge, sprawling faded yellow palazzo stood in the midst of ill-kept parkland. Its windows appeared to be boarded up, and it had the look of a ghost mansion slumbering in the sun.

"Is that Villa Carolina?" Margaret asked.

"No, it's Palazzo Ingranno," the driver said. "No one lives there now, but the old lady wanders through it, remembering the old days. The villa is off to the side near the garden. It used to be a hunting lodge or a pleasure house. Aldo says the big house is too much to care for, although the villagers hope he will restore it so that tourists will come to Ingranno and everybody gets rich. Aldo lives in the smaller place and looks after the gardens and the fountains himself. The laborers live in the village or in little farmhouses on the estate."

He turned into a pebbled drive that took them past another parallel driveway, which appeared to be abandoned and unusable due to a huge crater halfway up the hill. The sides of the crater were covered with a mat of weeds and spindly trees struggling to survive.

"Is the famous place where the *principessa* blew up the Germans," the driver said. "A small car can still drive it but is dangerous, and the *principessa* calls it 'the grave of my life,' so Aldo make a new drive."

Then they passed the palazzo and stopped in a circular courtyard at the entrance of a three-story house freshly painted yellow with bright white trim. Bright yellow, red, and orange flowers spilled out of stone urns, as slightly chipped statues of naked gods and warriors stood guard in the alcoves at either side of the door. A row of female statues with stone baskets balanced on their heads marched along the edge of the flat roof. A mossy fountain splashed in the center of the courtyard. Little marble putti on the edge of the basin held out their hands as if trying to grasp the sprays of water that shot into the air.

"I will return you to Rome before nightfall," the driver said.

An old woman all in black with the white apron of a servant opened the door.

"*Buon giorno*, Giulia!" the driver called out.

The old woman waved to him, then ushered Betty and Margaret into the villa. It turned out that she spoke no English, so Betty and Margaret sat where she indicated in a comfortable study to await Prince Aldo. Betty tried to spot the painting that Benedict was so eager to view, but the paintings on the walls were clearly of a later era: still lifes of dead animals and a couple of small landscapes that showed views of the distant St. Peter's. Tall vases of fresh flowers were artfully arranged, and the gold stamping on the leather books in the ceiling-high bookcases reflected the sun that entered through the windows. There was a glimpse of statuary and fountains from the windows, and carefully groomed parterres backed by a wall of ilexes and umbrella pines.

The black-clad Giulia brought them tiny cups of espresso and thin, crisp biscotti with almonds, but not enough to spoil their lunch. Betty understood her to say that *il principe* would be with them in five minutes.

Precisely five minutes later, Prince Aldo Castrocani entered the room. Margaret was impressed in spite of herself. There was a lot of Paul in his appearance, a fine Roman nose and dark brows. He was tall and slim in a well-cut suit, probably the new one that Paul had been so sure his father would acquire for the occasion. His hair was dark and somewhat long, with a faint tinge of silver at the temples. He definitely did not look like "the old boy," as Paul had referred to him, and when he smiled, he was devastatingly handsome.

"Lady Margaret, at last we meet. I have heard so

much about you in the few letters my boy manages to write." He had a slight and appealing accent. "And this must be Miss Trenka. Welcome to Villa Carolina." He looked around nervously as he spoke, then said softly, "My mother becomes upset when I use that name. To her it is still Villa Castrocani, as she never cared much for Carolyn Sue."

"We saw your mother today when we passed through the village," Betty said.

"It is a mild embarrassment to me for her to do the shopping, but she insists. She says the servants will take any old *pomodori* the sellers hand them and pay whatever is asked without bargaining. I suppose it keeps her engaged and active." He frowned slightly. "But she is not entirely stable in spite of a long rest in Switzerland, and I never really know what she is thinking. Well, enough of family concerns—or rather let us turn to other family concerns. Tell me what Paul is doing while I give you a tour of my garden. You won't find it too hot, Miss Trenka? I could have Giulia bring you a hat."

"I find it much cooler here than in Rome," Betty said, "and I have a policy against hats, but thank you. I'd love to see the garden."

"Are you a dedicated gardener then, Miss Trenka?"

"I'm afraid I have a gift for stunting the growth of plants, if not outright murdering them . . . ah . . . Prince . . ."

"Please call me Aldo. Titles are a source of pride only to my dear mother. She cares for nothing else except the palazzo, which to me is just a financial drain. I cannot afford to restore it properly. Our vineyards and olive trees provide for me, but alas not enough to restore frescoes and gold leaf and marble floors, and I cannot sell the property while my mother is still alive. It's been here since the sixteenth century, when our family left Rome for the country. If only Carolina were still my wife and willing to invest in restoring the palazzo. It has some fine features. Otherwise, I am happy here in my little villa." They left the villa and entered the garden through a freestanding marble arch.

"I understand you see Carolina often, Lady Margaret."

"Only as often as she comes to New York. About once a month. I seldom have the opportunity to travel to Dallas. She is well and seems happy."

"If Carolina has the material objects she desires, she is amazingly serene. And what of my boy?"

Margaret thought a moment. "Paul is very popular with New York society hostesses, so he goes about quite a bit, but he has not yet found work that satisfies him. He is otherwise well."

"I do not think any sort of work interests him," Aldo said. "I believe he prefers to live off the bounty of his mother. But the young woman he intends to marry, Georgina, may have a healthy influence on his ambition. He brought her to visit me, and I found her charming. Of course, she confided that Carolyn Sue is eager to plan a lavish wedding, which would not suit her. Carolina has always liked to take charge, even when the matter should not concern her. That tendency caused some friction in our marriage. Ah, come this way and allow me to show you my favorite spot." He led them around the green parterres and beds of flowers to a shady garden seat that looked down on an incline.

A narrow channel composed of regularly spaced whirls of carved stone made its way down the hill in what looked like gentle steps, ending at the bottom in an elaborate fountain in the middle of a still, square pool, and almost surrounded by a wall with lichen-covered statues in niches. Aldo fiddled with a metal key set in a carved block of stone and Betty saw a trickle of water start to flow at the top of the channel. It grew stronger until a rush of water swirled and foamed from one step to the next until it reached the pool at the bottom.

"It is called a water chain," Aldo said proudly. "There are of course, many finer examples in Italy— at Palazzo Farnese in Caprarola, at Villa Lante, and at Villa Aldobrandini over in Frascati, not far from here. The fountains at Villa d'Este are legendary. My chain is a modest device, but I love the sight of it."

Then the fountain in the pool came to life, spraying jets of water high into the air where they caught the sunlight to form little rainbows. The sound of flowing water was soothing.

Aldo closed his eyes and leaned back in the garden seat. "I come here every day to refresh my spirit," he said. "My mother has always thought the water chain to be a foolish conceit. It is not old enough for her. It was not built during the Renaissance when there was a great building boom in this area, but in modern times. I designed it myself, based on old plans, and installed it after the war. Of course, I had an engineer help with the design of the hydraulics. But Mamma prefers that everything remain as it always has. The twentieth century is far too recent for her. We'll come back here in the afternoon. Now Giulia must have our luncheon prepared. I hope my mother will feel up to joining us, but I warn you, she has little English, although I think she understands it quite well."

He gave one arm to Margaret and one to Betty to escort them back to the villa. Betty looked up at the top floor of the villa and thought she saw Princess Olympia's head of white hair at one of the windows. At least *someone* was there watching them, because the curtain fell back into place and the person was no longer visible.

The villa's dining room held a long table and comfortable chairs. Four places had been set with heavy silver and delicate wineglasses. Giulia stood at a sideboard and prepared to serve a huge antipasto. They took their seats, but the fourth place remained empty. Evidently the *principessa* had decided not to join them. The antipasto consisted of paper-thin slices of parmesan cheese and salami, a few tiny artichokes drizzled with olive oil, bright strips of red pepper, some chunks of tuna, and huge, fat black olives and bits of anchovies.

Beautiful little ravioli cut in the shape of mushrooms, filled with porcini and other mushrooms and sprinkled with truffles followed the antipasto. Then there were thin slices of veal, some rich red tomatoes, and slices of bread with olive oil for dipping.

"The oil is my very own," Aldo said. "We don't produce a great deal, but what there is of it is excellent." Giulia filled their wineglasses with a pale golden wine. "And this wine is from my grapes. Again, production is modest, but we harvest enough grapes to sell the extras to more serious vintners in the area."

As Giulia prepared to serve slices of cake and little cups of *gelato*, the dining room door was flung open and Principessa Olympia marched in. She glared at each of them in turn and then said something that sent Giulia scurrying away. Olympia wore an odd red turban on her hair and had swathed herself in a fringed cape of many colors. She had an unsteady hand with makeup, so the dark lining on her eyelids was not very precise, and she'd dabbed pink rouge liberally on each cheek. Lipstick did not follow the line of her lips. She looked like a demented gypsy fortune-teller.

"Mamma, this is m'lady Margaret from Inghilterra and Signora Trenka from America. Ladies, my mother, the Principessa Olympia Castrocani."

"How do you do?" Margaret and Betty said dutifully.

Olympia hissed.

"Mamma, Giulia has made her lovely mushroom ravioli for us. It's your favorite."

"*Favorita di* Carolina." This was said with considerable venom. She continued to speak, but Betty could not understand a word, although the tone was obvious. The princess was incensed about something. Mostly she addressed her tirade to Margaret, who looked quite taken aback, for she could speak more Italian than Betty.

"Mamma, Mamma," Aldo said helplessly. "Calm yourself."

Olympia turned her attention to Betty, who caught the words "*figlio e sposa*." *Son and wife*. Betty had not wasted her time listening to her Italian tapes. She could understand a few words of the language. Then Olympia said distinctly enough for Betty to understand, "*Madre, figlia e matrimonio*." *Mother, daughter, and marriage*. She pointed to Betty, then Margaret, and finally Aldo.

"No, no," Betty said, who thought she had grasped what Olympia was trying to convey, "Margaret is not my daughter. She is my friend, *amica*," but Olympia wasn't listening.

"Giulia, come here at once," Aldo said firmly as he frowned at his mother. Giulia crept back reluctantly, and Aldo instructed her to help his mother to her room. It took some persuading, but the two old ladies eventually departed.

"I apologize," Aldo said. "My mother has the impression that Lady Margaret has come here to marry me, much as Carolyn Sue did all those years ago, and will thus make changes to the villa and the palazzo, also as Carolyn Sue did, to my mother's distress. She further believes that you, Miss Trenka, are Lady Margaret's mother, who has put the idea of marriage into Margaret's head and is plotting to make it happen." He sighed. "Perhaps I should have left Mamma in Switzerland, but she missed the palazzo and the villa so much. I do hope you ladies are not offended."

"I am always being mistaken for someone I am not," Betty said. "A mother is just a new twist on an old theme."

"I am not at all offended," Margaret said. "Does she suspect that every female who visits has designs on you?"

"Only if they are young and blond. And foreign," Aldo said with a smile. "She will get over it after a little rest. Before the day is finished, I'll give you a glimpse of the palazzo. The entry hall is quite fine, but I am sorry to say that most of the furnishings are gone. But there are still some nice frescoes. . . ."

"I understand from various sources that you also have a painting of some note. . . ."

The prince sighed again. "That rumor will never die. Old Berenson heard something about it and came racing here from I Tatti, demanding to see it so he could authenticate it. Art students are always begging for a viewing. Dealers hound me."

"So it is not true?"

"Not exactly," he said slowly. "I do have one or two paintings that came here with my family in the early fifteen-hundreds. They had been done for the little palazzo we—my family, that is—once owned in Rome. It is now a government office. Such a pity. It was designed by one of the greatest architects of the Renaissance." Prince Aldo seemed to be avoiding the subject of the painting.

Margaret said, "So the painting is just a rumor?"

"You are as persistent as Carolina, who desperately hoped she'd have a masterpiece by a legendary artist to call her own. Yes, the picture does exist. Carolina begged me to have it authenticated by an expert, but I did not. It is in the style of Raphael. There is a date on it, a year or two before he died, so he could have painted it. He was living in Rome and laboring for the pope of the moment. I am fond of it, but the other works that are sometimes mentioned are definitely not Raphael's. The one Carolina wanted to be genuine was, I believe, probably painted in Raphael's workshop by an apprentice. Perhaps the design was the master's, but I don't think it is from his hand."

"Have you never consulted an expert?"

"I turned away Berenson, did I not? Possibly because I did not wish to know the truth. Perhaps one day when the vines fail and the olive trees are found to be diseased and I need a lot of money, I'll take the chance and ask an expert, but it is like the lottery. Many hope, but in the end few win. I prefer to hold on to the hope."

"There is a young man who happens to know Paul from the old days, an artist named Benedict Howe. He begged Betty and me to persuade you to allow him to see the painting. I made no promises, and I suggest you do not permit him to see it if he approaches you directly. He is likely to do so soon, because we saw him today in the little park below the palazzo. He is dishonest, possibly a forger. He associates with a gentleman named Josef Blum. . . ."

"The dealer. I know of him. He is one of those who have approached me about selling the picture. I understand his reputation is not good, although Piero Pannini swears by him. But Piero doesn't have the sense he was born with, so I pay him no attention. No, I will not allow Benedict Howe into my house. He was a rogue when he and Paul were friends. Paul fortunately did not sustain the friendship. The least I have done for my son is give him the ability to recognize an unsuitable companion. Now, let us tour the palazzo while Mamma is having her siesta."

CHAPTER 15

THE OLD palazzo was as ghostly inside as the exterior promised. Dust motes were heavy in the air, and the marble halls were empty. The first room they saw was very dim because the windows were covered with heavy if tattered curtains, but Margaret could see that the mosaic floor was quite beautiful. Birds and plants and butterflies made of colored bits of marble were intricately entwined in a pattern that covered the entire floor.

"The light in the next room is better," the prince said. "My mother has pulled back some of the curtains so the frescoes are visible in the sunlight. She comes here often, I suppose to remember the days when my father was alive. In those wartime days, this area was infested with German troops. The high command established its headquarters over in Frascati. The allies bombed the city badly as a result, but a lot of the high-ranking military men took over the villas around here for their personal use.

"They probably would have camped here in the palazzo, but before they had a chance to move in, my dear mother arranged with some of the partisans to obtain explosives, and when the lorry the Germans were riding in came up the old drive, she pushed a button at the right moment and they were all killed in the explosion. You can still see the spot where it happened."

"Ah, yes. We noticed the crater," Margaret said.

"I had to move the drive to its present location because the previous one was so torn up. My mother was . . . fearless. And determined. Of course, in the end, it was not a happy situation. The Germans massacred quite a few local men in retribution. I was just a baby at the time."

He did not mention that his father was one of those killed along with the other local men.

"My mother told me the story only once and never mentioned the affair again. Of course, I've heard it many times from people in the village and the *contadini* who work our farms. I believe those people would do anything for Mamma, because they admire her so greatly. And I believe that the sacrifice of my father after the explosion mitigated the grief of those who lost husbands and sons when the Germans retaliated."

He led them into the room with the frescoes. A small round skylight in the middle of the slightly domed ceiling provided enough light so that they could easily see the vast pictures of gods and goddesses, nymphs and satyrs that covered the walls and even the ceiling. A few graying marble busts stood on pedestals around the room, and there was a ratty chair and a sofa along one wall.

"Mamma likes to come here and sit alone, especially when it is stormy. She enjoys watching the dark clouds gather over the city and the rain washing away the dust." The window near the sofa afforded a view of distant Rome.

"There are many rooms upstairs," Aldo said, "but they are empty and uninteresting. The cellars below are like a labyrinth. There is even a corridor down there that connects to the cellar of my little villetta. I know where the door to the corridor is in the villa, but I was never able to find where it starts here in the palazzo. Come this way. The staircase is a marvel." He took them through a doorway and they found a splendid curving marble staircase leading to the upper floors.

"I am not sure who the architect was," Aldo said. "There are probably old records somewhere, but I've always thought he ought to have known that a grand staircase like that should have had a prominent place, visible to anyone who entered the palazzo." He shrugged. "Too late now to worry about it. It's been where it is for five hundred years. Now, ladies, I've been rushing you around and you'd probably like a little siesta after Giulia's fine meal."

"I wonder," Margaret said hesitantly, "if we might see the painting everyone else is so eager to view."

Aldo frowned slightly. Then he nodded. "I suppose it would be all right. I'd prefer, though, that you not talk about it to anyone, especially Mamma. It is a Madonna, and Mamma loves it for its religious meaning. She is very devout and traditional.

In fact, when she came into luncheon today, it was the first time I had seen her wear any color other than black. She has dressed in black since she was widowed, without fail."

"I think," Betty said, "that she might have been making a statement of some sort regarding the young, blond, foreign woman who is visiting her son."

She was relieved to hear him laugh. "Competing for my attention, perhaps?"

They strolled back in the direction of the villa. The grass of the park in front of the palazzo was in need of cutting, and the scattered statues were mossy with lichen.

"So much needs to be done," Aldo said. "But there's a sturdy ancient." He pointed to a gnarled old olive tree. "It really doesn't belong in this setting, but it has been here forever. Mamma wouldn't allow me to remove it, even though it's out of place in the park. She says that it was here when my great-great-grandfather was alive, so here it stays until a wind topples it. As a boy, when I was naughty, I used to climb it to hide away among the leaves until my misbehavior was forgotten, and Paul did as well.

"The villagers swear that it is more than five hundred years old, planted when the palazzo was built. It still bears olives, but not many. Giulia saves them for curing to eat with the antipasto. The fruit from the rest of my trees, less than a hundred now, is pressed for olive oil. Years ago we had our own *frantoio* here on the estate to press the olives, but we make little of our own oil these days. Instead what olives we harvest go to the *frantoio comunale* to be pressed with the olives of the other growers. The industry is not as extensive in this area as it is in Tuscany. Most growers concentrate on wine grapes."

Suddenly they heard a hissing sound from behind a trellis covered with a tangle of pink roses. Then Principessa Olympia emerged, now again dressed entirely in black and muttering what sounded like curses directed at Margaret and Betty.

Aldo went to her and spoke softly. Returning to Betty and Margaret, he said, "I asked her why she wasn't enjoying a siesta, and she said that the *ragazzi* were keeping her awake. She finally told them to run off and hide in the old olive tree or she would have to punish them. There are no boys here." He shrugged. "I hope she is not hearing voices and imagining things as she did before I put her under care in Switzerland. Also, she is not pleased that you two are still here. I'll have Giulia take her to the palazzo and settle her on her sofa to calm down. That way she will not interfere when I show you our painting."

"Who do you suppose the boys she mentioned are?" Margaret asked.

"Children of the *contadini* perhaps. Children make Mamma nervous. Paul made her nervous, although as a boy he was good about not annoying her. Only now and then did she send him to the olive tree to get him out of her sight." Giulia came into view, as if she knew she was needed, and took Olympia to the palazzo.

"I think Margaret is wondering whether the boys

might be Benedict Howe and Max Grey," Betty said.

"I see. I'll have Luca, my driver, have a look around to see if they are anywhere about. But how could they have encountered Mamma? She would be very suspicious of foreigners on her property, and I do not believe she was in residence when Paul brought Benedict to this place years ago."

"Tell Luca that Max has a very flashy red sports car. Easily noticed," Betty said. "And as for meeting those boys, your mother might have encountered them in the park down the hill as she was returning from the village on foot. They are clever enough to have found out who she is. They both speak Italian well and might have tried to persuade her to facilitate a viewing of the painting. That seems to be the only thing on Benedict's mind."

"Which would not have pleased her," Aldo said. "Perhaps her concern about the picture and their demands to see it made her uneasy. That might be what she meant about the *ragazzi* keeping her awake. She has never allowed anyone to see it, although I did take Carolina to look at it without Mamma's knowledge. It is partly at Mamma's urging that I refuse all requests. She has access to it, but it is quite safely locked up."

He motioned for them to follow him around the side of the palazzo. While the façade was well maintained, the walls that were not visible from the village and the road below were in need of paint. The windows were dusty and the trim chipped and grimy. The grass in some places was ankle high, while the stones set in the ground to form a walk-way had not seen an edger for years.

Still, here on the hidden side of the palazzo were several neatly kept flowerbeds featuring climbing roses and yet another fountain, this one inactive, merely a marble faun set in the middle of a mossy basin filled with murky water.

All the way around on the opposite side of the palazzo, set on the side of the hill and quite near Aldo's villa, was a curious little detached building made of greenish marble streaked with white. Betty noticed a small golden cross on the peak of the roof and surmised that it was a private family chapel. Then she noticed a statue of the Virgin Mary stand-ing in the midst of a circular flowerbed planted with white climbing roses on low trellises.

A Christian chapel indeed, for there were no Greek and Roman gods and goddesses in evidence, and the single window Betty spotted high above the door seemed to be a stained-glass scene of saints and angels. The brass fittings on the wooden door were well polished and the steps up to the door were swept clean of leaves.

"I am not sure that the chapel has maintained its consecrated status," Aldo said as he unlocked the door with a large key, meanwhile pressing three or four buttons on a small electronic alarm box at-tached to the door. "In the very old days, of course, the priest would walk up from the village and cele-brate Mass for the Castrocanis, but those days are long gone. My mother uses the chapel now for her private devotions, but she walks down the hill to the church in the village for Sunday Mass, confession, and holy day services. The priest is almost as old as she but not as active, so he prefers not to make the trip here."

"Is this where you keep the painting?" Margaret asked.

"It seems safest here. I feel the security is good. Besides the locks, there is an alarm system that my mother sometimes forgets to disengage. If it sounds, though, I can hear it in the villa, as can Luca in his rooms over the garage. Since the chapel is mostly marble and not attached to other buildings, it makes it less likely to be involved should there be a fire in the palazzo or the villa."

CHAPTER 16

THE CHAPEL was dark, illuminated only by little pools of colored light that dotted the slippery marble floor from the rose window above the door. The place smelled of dust and beeswax. A few chairs with kneelers in the middle of the chapel faced a long table covered with a red cloth and flanked by massive candlesticks nearly the height of a man. Each held a fat white candle dripping with hardened wax. On either side of the chapel were alcoves framed by columns of colored marble. In one was a statue of a saint before which was a row of votive candles. Only one was lit and the flame flickered faintly, about to drown in melted wax. A bouquet of drooping flowers had been placed at the saint's feet in a large, somewhat dirty vase of heavy glass.

"I have told Mamma not to leave candles burning," Aldo sighed as he doused the flame, and directed them to another alcove, opposite the first and blocked by a railing and another stand of votive candles. They could see a gold frame on the wall, but dark curtains covered whatever was in the frame.

When Aldo flipped a switch attached to one of the columns, a faint light came on above the frame and shone down on the curtains. He then punched in a code on the keypad of another alarm device. He finally stepped through a gate in the railing guarding the alcove and approached the frame, pulling a golden cord so that the curtains opened to reveal a painting of a Madonna, dressed in blue robes with a filmy red scarf dangling above a plump, smiling Christ child and another naked plump little boy who held a plain cross made of thin sticks. The smile on the Madonna's tilted head was sober but sweet as she gazed down at her son. The background was a scene of lush vegetation against a pale blue sky.

"Mary and Jesus with Saint John the Baptist," Aldo said. "Each time I look at the painting, I am convinced that it is a real Raphael. I have viewed most of the authenticated Raphael Madonnas in Italy, France, England, and the United States, and while the composition of this one is not exactly like any of the others, there is a degree of similarity. Perhaps I was wrong not to allow Berenson to examine it and offer his opinion, but I did not care for his arrogance. And then again, he might have decreed it to be less than I wished it to be." He looked at Margaret almost pleadingly. "Was I a coward?" Betty wondered if he was flirting with her.

Margaret smiled at him sympathetically. Perhaps she was flirting with him. "It's a beautiful picture, and does it matter so much whose hand painted it?"

"I suppose not. Mamma comes here often to pray

before it. She has even made a little bed for herself here behind the railing, just a pile of blankets, so that she can hold private all-night vigils in the chapel. I have forbidden her to do so, but no Italian mother feels it necessary to obey a mere son."

"Did Paul come here often?" Margaret asked.

"He was free to go anywhere, and when he was older and living in Rome, I believe he liked the chapel. As a boy, he was not allowed here alone, because of the possible value of the picture." Aldo grinned. "He was not a very religious little boy. Carolyn Sue, coming from that Texas Southern Baptist world, did not exactly encourage devotion to the Roman Church. It was one of the things that set my mother against her."

Betty moved away from them and looked around the chapel. If they were engaged in flirtation, she didn't want to interfere by her presence. A few other paintings of religious subjects hung about the chapel, but she didn't know enough about art to identify their school, and certainly not the artist. After a time, she sat on one of the chairs facing the simple altar and recalled her young days when she had been firmly bound to her religion, although none of the churches she'd attended had had the same architectural and artistic quality as this structure from the High Renaissance.

Saint Mary's, where her family had worshiped, was a squat building of pale brownish stone, with an awkward bell tower and many pious pictures of the saints. She sometimes envied the Connecticut Yankees of her town their spacious and gracious tall-steepled white churches, but she never said anything to Ma and Pop, who distrusted the contaminating influence even of Betty's friendship with the little Congregationalist girls who were near neighbors.

She glanced over her shoulder at Aldo and Margaret, who were both gazing up at the alleged Raphael, and it seemed to her that their hands were touching. Perhaps Principessa Olympia did have reason to fear that this young, foreign, blond woman had designs on the prince.

Suddenly Margaret was at her side. "I'm finding it a bit stuffy in here, so we both would like to leave," she said. "Aldo says that you can stay as long as you wish. He'll leave the curtains over the painting open so you can have another look at it. Just tell him at once when you leave. He wants to be sure the chapel is secure for the night. You can find us at the villa. He has ordered the car for us at eight, if that is all right with you."

"I might just sit here for a time, and let you two young people talk about Mrs. Hoopes and Prince Paul. Then I'll join you in a while."

"Aldo doesn't seem interested in reliving his past with Carolyn Sue," Margaret said. "In fact, he seems more intent on interesting me in him. Ah, Italian men are one of a kind."

"Or all of a kind," Betty said. "Don't let his mother catch on."

Margaret and the prince were laughing as they left the chapel arm-in-arm. Betty heard the heavy door thump shut, leaving her alone in the dimness.

It was very quiet and peaceful. She walked over to the painting and stood before it, trying to memorize its details so as to be able to describe it to Ted when she was back in Connecticut and they were settled in at his house over a cup of his good coffee.

Suddenly Betty froze. She heard a sound as though someone was shuffling softly across on the marble floor. Mice, perhaps, or the petals of the dried flowers in the vase near the saint falling to the ground. Or it could be Olympia, ready to defend her beloved Madonna. Then she heard the door squeak, and saw a sliver of daylight as it opened. She huddled close to one of the columns as the door swung wide and someone entered the chapel. Aldo hadn't locked the door when he and Margaret left, so it could be anyone who cared to turn the knob and come in. Aldo's mother now willing to show Benedict and Max the picture? Or the boys alone, and who knew what they would do when they saw her? Anyone. She held her breath and felt her heart pounding.

"Miss Trenka?" She felt weak with relief at the sound of Prince Aldo's voice. He came to her side. "I hope I didn't alarm you, but Giulia says that Mamma has been in a terrible state. She saw you and me and Margaret entering the chapel. I was afraid to leave you here alone, because I don't know what she might do if she decided you should not be here in her special place. Come along with me now. Margaret and I are having an *aperitivo* at the water chain."

"That might be a good idea," Betty said. "It's a bit scary here, if I may say so."

Aldo proceeded to draw the curtains on the painting, set the alarm, turn off the light, and usher her through the door. He paused to turn the key and reset the alarm there before leaving, and led the way to the spot overlooking the water chain and the fountain where Margaret was enjoying the view.

"I suppose your mother still believes that I am Margaret's mother."

"We don't know exactly what my mother thinks," the prince said. "But she remains very protective of me and her possessions," Betty said.

When Betty was settled in a chair, Giulia brought them icy glasses of *granita*, coffee-flavored crushed ice, then paused to whisper something to the prince. He raised his eyebrows at whatever she said, and stood.

"If you ladies will forgive me, I have something urgent to attend to." He bowed slightly and hurried away with Giulia.

"I hope the *principessa* hasn't done something unexpected," Margaret said. Then she stood up. "I think I'll wander down the slope a bit and view the water chain from a different angle. I like the way the water bounces off the carvings and leaps down to the next level."

She left Betty sitting peacefully with her glass of *granita* and made her way along the informal path that bordered the splashing water in its channel. After a moment, she was hidden by the carefully trimmed bushes. The silence was broken only by the soothing sounds of flowing water. Betty closed her eyes and actually fell into a doze. A sound behind her startled her into wakefulness, but for a moment she was confused about where she was.

Just as she remembered, a large hand slapped a damp cloth across her nose and mouth, and she smelled a sharp medicinal odor before she faded away into near unconsciousness. She heard someone speaking rapid Italian, then felt herself being lifted by someone who must have been quite strong because she was a large, tall woman, not a delicate package by any means. She lost track of reality as she was carried away, although she was certain that there were at least two others accompanying her in addition to the person who carried her. Before they reached wherever they were headed, she gave herself up to sleep. She didn't struggle because her limbs felt as heavy as iron.

She was unaware of being dumped on a soft pile of something, and didn't hear the voices of her abductors. Then, for a moment, jolted to semi-consciousness by a shout of triumph, she did hear something. Next there was the sound of a scuffle, a woman's voice speaking angry Italian, and finally a sharp cry of pain and a moan. Then silence. She strained to hear if her abductors were still about, but she slipped again into semiconsciousness. She slept.

CHAPTER 17

WHEN MARGARET returned from viewing the water chain, she found only Betty's glass lying in the grass, with no indication of where Betty herself had gone. She decided that Betty must have found it too hot outdoors and returned to the villa.

As she made her way through the neat garden toward the villa, she noticed a man standing in the overgrown parkland near the old olive tree, gazing out at the distant city. For a moment, she thought it was Josef Blum, but decided she was mistaken. But when she reached the main door of the villa, she was surprised to see a dark maroon sedan parked in the circular drive in front of the entrance and decided that an unexpected arrival had been the cause of Prince Aldo's sudden departure. Perhaps it actually was Josef Blum paying a call, and the man she'd seen had been Blum after all. The front door was locked, and when she pulled the old-fashioned bell cord to summon Giulia, it was quite some time before anyone responded. It was not Giulia but Prince Aldo himself who opened the door.

"I wonder if Miss Trenka returned to the villa,"

Margaret said, a little nervously. "She might have been taken ill from the rich lunch or too much sun and walking about."

"I left her with you. Is she not still there?"

"I walked down the incline a ways to look at the fountain, and when I returned, she was gone."

Prince Aldo frowned. "I will ask Giulia and Mamma if they have seen her, but I do not believe she is in the villa. Although others are. Do you know a Mr. and Mrs. Flood? They claim to be acquainted with you."

"The Floods? Here? What on earth do they give as a reason?"

"It is not altogether clear. Something about the young man named Benedict Howe, who wants so much to see my Madonna."

"The very same. We know he is in Ingranno, because Betty and I saw him in the park, remember? With Max Grey."

"Mr. Flood appears to be upset about something, or possibly everything. Mrs. Flood herself is not totally in control of her emotions. I do not understand what is going on. You must try to talk to them, but we must first find Miss Trenka. She may have wandered off in the gardens. There is a small labyrinth carved out of hedges, but it would take a very . . . um . . . careless person to become hopelessly lost in it. I do not feel that Miss Trenka is careless. Still, we should take a look. Giulia will go through the rooms here in case she entered the villa unnoticed and lay down somewhere for a siesta. And I'll send Luca to check the labyrinth and the gardens."

"Perhaps I should speak with the Floods now to find out what they are up to," Margaret said. "I don't like their sudden appearance here, not with Benedict in the vicinity."

She explained to the prince about the painting Benedict was to do of Phyllis, in the style of the Renaissance, with an authentic Italian background, and about the apparent intimacy between the two and Lester's justifiable annoyance in the matter.

"I believe that Lester attempted to shoot Benedict back in England. He is rather hotheaded."

"They were accompanied here by Josef Blum," Prince Aldo said, "although I do not know where he is at the moment. This so-called artist, Benedict Howe, is not in the party. It seems that Signor Blum has tempted Mr. Flood with the possibility of acquiring my Raphael, and he is demanding to see the painting. I have refused, naturally, and told them it is not for sale. Ah, Giulia, have you seen Signora Trenka in the villa?"

Giulia shook her head.

"Then find Luca and the two of you search the grounds. She might have fallen and injured herself."

Just then the prince's mother appeared in a doorway and unleashed a stream of angry Italian in their direction.

The prince actually smiled. "It seems that my mother does not approve of the Floods. She says they are disrespectful of the villa and the palazzo. I told you that Mamma understands more English than she will admit to."

He spoke a few words to her that seemed to calm

her, but then Margaret heard him say something about "Signora Trenka," and the old lady returned to high-speed, high-decibel Italian. Prince Aldo shrugged.

"She seems to have taken a great dislike to the woman she believes is your mother, Lady Margaret. She continues to blame her for trying to orchestrate a marital relationship between you and me, and nothing I say can change her mind. Let me take you to Mr. and Mrs. Flood. Then I'll join the search for Miss Trenka."

The Floods were sitting stiffly on the edges of antique chairs in a drawing room, as far from each other as possible. The prince didn't accompany Margaret into the room, merely opening the door for her before disappearing down a hallway.

"What on earth are you two doing at Villa Carolina? And where is Josef Blum?" Margaret asked not quite pleasantly. She was beginning to worry about Betty, and the sight of the Floods didn't improve her mood.

"Joe went outside to take a look at the view. Ben said it was perfectly okay to drop in," Phyllis said almost tearfully. "He said tourists and art lovers were always popping in unannounced to see the art. He said Prince Castrocani didn't mind at all."

Just then, Josef Blum made his appearance, and ignoring Margaret, began to circle the drawing room, examining the paintings on the walls as though he were a vulture checking on whether a carcass was ripe for feeding.

"I shouldn't think anyone would go a step out of

his way to look at this junk," Blum said. "None of it is of any value whatsoever." When Margaret merely stared at him, he returned to his examination of the pictures.

"I believe the prince does mind surprise visitors, Phyllis," Margaret said. "This is not a museum, but a private residence. And how does it happen that you arranged to visit while Miss Trenka and I are here—by invitation, I assure you."

Phyllis fidgeted, but a sullen Lester said, "Joe said you would surely be allowed to see the important painting, and we could ride in on your coattails, as it were. I want that picture, and I can afford it. But I like to see what I'm buying before I hand over the cash. Joe's a respected art dealer, so the prince wouldn't turn him down."

"And what role does Benedict play in this scheme?"

"No role. He just made the suggestion."

"But he's here, of course."

Lester shrugged. "He could be. He and Phyl have been cooking things up since they met. I'd like to see that little weasel hung up by his . . . his palette knife."

"He's a nice boy, Les," Phyllis said. "I don't know why you've taken against him so."

Josef Blum joined them. "He's a very talented young man, and he and Max are delightful companions. Lady Margaret, can't you persuade Prince Aldo to allow us just a glimpse of the painting?"

"He keeps it well hidden," Margaret said, "and I have absolutely no influence. . . ."

"But the old *principessa* told me that you and the prince were contemplating marriage," Blum said smugly. "She was very certain about this, although I don't think she approves."

"She is entirely wrong," Margaret said. "I barely know the man, and besides, he was once married to one of my best friends. I think the old *principessa* suffers from delusions. When did you see her to hear this?"

Again, Blum ignored Margaret.

"And where is your Miss Trenka?" Phyllis asked. "Such a nice old lady, who definitely does not suffer from delusions."

"I think she would not care to be referred to as a 'nice old lady,' " Margaret said. "I don't believe she can be much more than a decade older than Carolyn Sue Hoopes."

Phyllis looked puzzled, so Margaret said, "Prince Aldo's former wife. I thought certainly you'd know her."

Phyllis had a practiced, artificial laugh. "Oh, Carolyn *Sue*. I misheard you. Dear Carol. That old?"

Fortunately, Lester's impatience halted discussion of Carolyn Sue's age. "Joe, I've just got to see that picture. Now, where's that scumbag Ben? He said he'd be here before us, and he promised I'd get a look. And where's this prince anyhow?" The sarcasm was evident.

"Perhaps Phyllis knows where Ben is. I last saw him out in the garden with Max," Blum said.

Good grief, Margaret thought, the whole tribe is here—Ben and Max and the Floods and Blum. This is too much. And where is Betty?

Betty, as it happened, wasn't sure herself where she was or how long she had been there. Her head throbbed, and when she tried to sit up, she was overcome with dizziness, so she lay back until the spinning stopped. Wherever she was, it was quite dark, but her eyes soon adjusted, and immediately she knew that she was lying on the pile of blankets in the chapel, the *principessa*'s makeshift bed.

She looked up at the spot where the painting hung, but all she saw was the gilt frame with the protective curtains torn away and dangling by a few shreds of cloth. Where the painting had been was just a bare piece of wood. Then she froze at the sound of a low moan. Carefully she crawled to the railing that divided the niche from the rest of the chapel. She could see a flickering votive candle on the other side of the chapel, and lying on the floor in a spot of color from the stained-glass window above the door was a lump of black cloth. Principessa Olympia surely. What had happened?

Fighting a wave of nausea, she attempted to stand again and finally made it to her feet. If the old lady was moaning, at least she was alive. Betty's knees were weak and her head continued to spin as she moved carefully across the floor to the sprawled body. It was an effort to kneel down and examine the woman, who appeared to have been struck on the head. There was a wound on her temple seeping blood, but it didn't appear to be serious. Still, she was very old, and any injury could be life-threatening. Betty looked around. She thought she remembered a holy water font near the door. She found a clean handkerchief in her pocket and limped toward the font, then returned to Olympia and dabbed at the cut with the damp cloth. The *principessa* moaned again and opened her eyes.

She muttered something in Italian that Betty didn't understand, then she heard "*Ragazzi...*" *Boys.* Benedict and Max? Betty looked around, but the boys were not in evidence. If they had been here, they must be responsible for the empty picture frame. Then Olympia tried to sit up, finally managing to do so with Betty's help. She was clutching the heavy glass vase that had held the saint's flowers, which were strewn about the floor. She pantomimed swinging the vase and Betty understood that she had tried to defend her beloved painting from the two who were bent on stealing it. In return, they had struck her down and departed with the painting.

She helped Olympia move to a column guarding the saint's alcove and left her propped up against it while she decided what to do next. Help for the *principessa* seemed the first order of business. And herself. She was feeling quite unwell but could not remember clearly how she came to be here. She tried the door, but it was locked, and she wished she knew how to activate the alarm. That would bring someone to their aid. Surely Margaret would have noticed that she was missing. She joined Olympia and leaned against the pillar to rest. Perhaps the prince would soon think to check the chapel.

Back at the villa, Margaret said carefully, "The prince is searching for Miss Trenka, who seems to have disappeared."

Phyllis was also adept at artificial shock and disbelief. Then she said maliciously, "Old people are often forgetful and tend to wander off." Margaret was certain that if Betty had been present to hear that, she would have cheerfully cracked Phyllis sharply across the mouth.

"You are being ageist, Mrs. Flood," Josef Blum said. "I spent a very pleasant evening with Miss Trenka, and I did not detect the slightest sign that she was muddled or prone to wandering off. Niccolo Orsini found her delightful."

Prince Aldo reappeared, followed by Giulia and Luca. "We can find no sign of Miss Trenka or my mother anywhere. We are now going to search the palazzo. Mr. Flood, would you care to assist us?"

"Why, sure I'll help," Lester said. He glanced at Phyllis and Blum, who both avoided his look. "We'll just wait for you outside in the sunshine. Great place you've got here, prince. Come on, Phyl, Joe." The three of them departed to enjoy the sunshine.

"Before you go, Aldo," Margaret said, "could I speak with you privately? I have an idea."

"Of course, Margaret." He led her to a distant corner of the room, although there was no one to overhear them.

"Elizabeth may have decided to view the water chain from below, as I did. Have you looked there?"

"I glanced down the hill, but I saw no one. I will send Giulia and Luca with those people to look in the palazzo while you and I look along the water chain and the area around it. I do not have much hope, however. I found outside . . ." He fumbled in the pocket of his elegant suit and took out a piece of paper. "It appears to be a ransom note. It suggests that someone has taken Miss Trenka hostage."

Margaret was so startled by the news that she sank into the nearest chair.

"There are terms for her safe return: I must hand over the painting itself. She will be returned safely if I also promise that you and she will leave Villa Carolina immediately and not return. Does that ransom not suggest that Benedict Howe is the culprit?"

"Or just about anyone else here at the moment. The promise about us leaving, however, suggests that your mother played a role. Wait, that paper looks familiar." She examined the note carefully. "It looks very much like the paper sliced from one of our old books at Priam's Priory, and Benedict is certainly the culprit in that theft. But, Aldo, I think Elizabeth would strongly object to being ransomed, especially if it cost you your painting."

"Then what am I to do, *cara*?"

"I wonder . . . could she be hidden in the chapel?"

"Impossible. Only I and Mamma can enter. Benedict and this Max could not get past the security."

"Unless they persuaded your mother to open the door, which she might well do if it meant that she'd be rid of poor Betty, whom she so clearly loathes."

"Quickly, then, let us survey the water chain to be sure she is not there, and then go on to the chapel."

They walked through the fading light of the day to the water chain, which still gushed down the incline. Prince Aldo turned the key to halt the flow and they looked down the hill. The fountain in the midst of the pool was still shooting jets of water into the air. Suddenly Aldo grasped Margaret's arm. "There is something amiss. Look, down there in the fountain. Come."

He helped her down the hill to the big fountain and pool at the bottom.

"What is it?" Margaret asked, but the question was simply rhetorical. *It* was the body of a man floating facedown in the murky pool with the spray from the fountain splashing down on him.

"It seems to be a dead person," Aldo said, "and a preliminary observation suggests that it is Benedict Howe. I can't be certain, but . . . look there."

He pointed to a bundle of papers on the grass at the edge of the fountain. They raced down the hill, slipping and stumbling until they reached the fountain. Aldo snatched up the papers and unrolled them.

"Sketches of my Madonna and some others of pictures I do not recognize. Very nicely done, all of them. He did find a way into the chapel after all. And look." Propped up against a small bush was a board a couple of feet square. He turned it over. It was the painting of the Madonna. "Not as much damage as there would have been had it been painted on canvas, and he cut it from the frame and rolled it up."

"Someone must have killed him in order to take the sketches and the painting," Margaret said. "But they were left here. That's curious. How was he killed? And shouldn't we try to retrieve the body? I mean, in case he's not actually dead."

"If I am not mistaken, that is a knife protruding from his back, possibly the very knife he used to pry the board from the frame. The handle of the knife looks like the kind the vineyard workers use, a big blade that could cut an aorta or puncture a lung if plunged into the back. He seems very dead to me, but yes, we must get him out of the fountain. It is not very deep. I can wade out to him."

Margaret almost felt the pain that crossed Prince Aldo's face as he removed his shoes and waded into the fountain in his elegant new suit. The water in the pool came almost to his knees and the spray from the fountain drenched his jacket.

"Who could have done this?" Margaret asked as Aldo dragged the body to the edge of the fountain and heaved it up over the rim onto dry ground. "Blum wanted the picture. Lester wanted it. The kidnappers wanted it. That would be Max and Ben, logically."

"And I wanted it to remain where it was."

They looked at each other, not daring to speak the name of the one other person who definitely wanted the Madonna to remain where it had always been.

"Impossible," Aldo said finally. "My mother is a passionate woman, but she is old and not strong. She could not have killed him."

Just then, he spotted Luca walking away from the palazzo and summoned him with a shout and a wave. Luca came running. "I do not know how the local authorities will handle this," Aldo said, indicating the body at the edge of the pool, "but Luca must fetch them. As a dedicated communist, he does not think much of the police, but he will do what is necessary."

"Ah," Luca said in disgust when he saw Benedict's body. "What is this?"

"Someone has murdered this creature," Prince Aldo said. "Not much of a loss, but we must attend to him. Go down to the village and see if the constabulary can put aside his evening glass of wine and join us here. Fetch the doctor as well." Luca started away. "Did you find Signora Trenka in the palazzo?"

"No one is there, *principe*. Not even your mother."

"Ah, yes. My mother. Hurry to Ingranno, and do not stop to advertise this business to the villagers."

Prince Aldo looked down wistfully at his soaked trousers, then flicked droplets of water from the fountain from his jacket and bravely squared his shoulders.

"Should we not visit the chapel to see what other damage he might have done?" Margaret asked.

"You are most practical, Margaret. I like that in a woman."

CHAPTER 18

P_{RINCE} A_{LDO} placed the painting carefully on the grass and covered it with the sheets of drawings he had found. "As soon as Luca returns, I will carry the painting to the villa where it will always be under my eye. I still wonder who was able to murder the boy."

Margaret said, "Almost no one was out and about alone, not the Floods anyhow, but I saw Blum near the olive tree when I was going to the villa to find Betty. Then Blum came into the villa soon after I met the Floods there. So Phyllis and Lester had no time or opportunity to do this awful thing, but Blum did. He definitely wanted the painting, but I don't see him kidnapping Betty to get it. On the other hand, if Ben had already stolen it, I don't think Blum would hesitate to appropriate it for himself, even if it involved murder. But of course, he would be murdering his special forger who probably earned him a lot of money. Then there's Max, but what reason could he have? . . ."

"Money again," the prince said.

"Right," Margaret said. "He could have forced

Blum to pay for the painting, so Blum could resell it, with his authentication, to the likes of the Floods, probably for more than he would give Max."

"But the painting is still here. If the murder was committed because of the painting, it was to no avail." Suddenly the alarm in the chapel clanged loudly and a sharp siren pierced the air. Without hesitation, Margaret and Aldo raced toward the building.

Prince Aldo had the key to the chapel in his hand to unlock the door. Then he silenced the alarm. "Someone—and that could only be my mother—opened the chapel for the thief. And I believe that must have been Benedict, because he's the one who's dead."

He pushed open the door and they entered the dimness cautiously. Nothing moved in the chapel, although they saw that the votive candle at the foot of the saint's statue had been lighted.

"Look!" Margaret raced to the two women who were leaning against the column. "Elizabeth, are you all right?"

"A little worse for wear," Betty said, "but the *principessa* has been hurt. I couldn't understand her, but she did mention boys, the *ragazzi*, again. And the painting is gone. It must have been Benedict and Max who made her open the chapel after they kidnapped me, and then they stole the painting. I believe she tried to stop them, and they hit her. They merely chloroformed me while I was waiting at the water chain and dumped me here. When I woke up, I tried to help the *principessa* and then found the alarm box here and pushed every button until it went off."

"Mamma, Mamma," the prince crooned, and Olympia's eyes fluttered open. She put her hand to her injured head. "Luca will bring the doctor, if he doesn't stop along the way to discuss Marxism with Ingranno's masses."

"At least we have Betty back without paying the ransom," Margaret said. "Perhaps your mother should lie down until a doctor comes."

"I'll bring her the blankets," Betty said. "I spent a few hours on them unconscious." She stopped and looked back. "What ransom?"

"You in exchange for the painting," Margaret said, "which leads us to believe that Ben and Max and possibly your beau, Josef Bloom, were involved."

Betty grinned. "If it's a genuine Raphael, I'm sure I'm not worth it. I hope you two weren't going to give in to the demand."

"We think," Margaret said, "that the princess might also have had a hand in your kidnapping. Besides the painting, they wanted a guarantee that you and I would leave immediately, never to return."

"We didn't have to consider paying the ransom," Aldo said. "We found Benedict Howe dead in the pool at the foot of the water chain. Stabbed in the back by an unknown murderer. The painting was nearby. Margaret, the painting! We left it behind when we heard the chapel alarm. I must retrieve it." Aldo rushed away.

"Hmm. The murderer is probably not entirely unknown," Betty said.

"I don't really think Josef Blum had the time or opportunity," Margaret said. "The Floods certainly didn't. Oh yes, they're all here," she said in response to Betty's look of surprise. "Just dropped from the sky right before you disappeared. Benedict and Max instructed them to come. Those boys certainly had time to connive with the princess to arrange your kidnapping and to steal the painting—and for Max to do Ben in."

A short time later, Aldo returned with empty hands and a sad expression. "It wasn't where I left it," he said. "I don't know what to do next, except to apologize to Miss Trenka. When I spoke to my mother just now, she admitted that she had arranged with those boys to have you kidnapped. As the ransom note indicated, she wanted you and Margaret to go away so you would forget about trying to get me to marry your 'daughter.' Benedict and Max came up with the idea of the kidnapping so as to gain access to the painting and at least make sketches of it, so they talked Mamma into opening the chapel in exchange for getting rid of you.

"I assume that Benedict would have attempted to pass off the sketches as preliminary drawings for the painting. Or handed them over to Blum to unload them. They could be worth a lot if the picture was authenticated. Mamma thought that kidnapping Miss Trenka was an excellent idea, but she turned against the boys when she saw Benedict removing her painting. She tried to stop him and Max, but one of them hit her and they made off with the picture. She swears she did not shove a knife in Benedict's back, although she would have liked to do it."

"But someone did, and likely it was Max," Betty said. "Where do you suppose he's gone? Back to Rome?"

"Without the painting? I think not," Aldo said. "But if Max was the person who made off with it when Margaret and I heard the alarm and ran to the chapel, he may still be somewhere around the estate until he feels it's safe to get away. The villa would be a poor hiding place, but perhaps he is in the palazzo."

"What if Lester Flood is the murderer? He failed to kill Ben in England, but maybe he succeeded here. While he was out enjoying the sunshine, he saw Ben with the picture and decided he wanted it enough to kill for it. And as long as we're speculating, the same is true of Josef Blum, who would have had plenty of time for murder." Margaret seemed quite pleased with her theories.

"It couldn't have been Lester. Phyllis was with him, and she certainly wouldn't have allowed him to kill her dear Ben," Betty said. "Should we not gather everyone together, so that Josef or the Floods won't help Max escape with the painting?"

"I think I should stay here with Mamma until the doctor arrives," Aldo said. "Giulia and the others are searching the palazzo for Miss Trenka."

"We'll go there," Margaret said, "if Betty feels able, and change the object of the search from Betty to Max."

"I'm all right," Betty said. "I wasn't treated

roughly, and my headache is going away." But she didn't offer more comments as she and Margaret walked toward the palazzo. They could see a dusty sort of ambulance making its way slowly up the hill from the village, preceded by what appeared to be a police vehicle.

"Luca seems to have done his job," Margaret said. "I hope the *principessa* wasn't badly damaged in defending the picture. Did you hear anything that went on?"

Betty stopped, closed her eyes, and concentrated. "I heard male voices," she said. "I think they were Ben and Max. They mentioned Josef and the car, the panel and Rome. I heard Olympia shriek and moan when she was attacked. I was too knocked out to know exactly what was said, but it may come back to me. Only Benedict and Max would have been strong enough to haul me off to the chapel." Then she said suddenly, "If it was Max who murdered Benedict, he would try to get away from here at once. I wonder if Max's little red car is still down below near the park. It would be the perfect way to escape Ingranno. Can we see the car park from up here?"

"I think we can look down at it from the main door to the palazzo," Margaret said. "Let's have a go at it." As they walked toward the palazzo, a mini-swarm of police and medical personnel emerged from the vehicles. Luca was busily directing them toward the water chain and the fountain. Margaret waved to gain his attention, then shouted through cupped hands, "*La principessa, la cappella. Rapidamente.*"

Luca acknowledged her and herded some of his troops toward the chapel.

"Well, she'll get some medical attention now," Margaret said. She peered down the hill. "How odd. The red car is still there, so Max must not have taken the easiest opportunity to escape. I do hope he's not holed up in the palazzo. I'm sure Josef would help him elude capture, and given what Max did to you and the princess, he's probably dangerous."

"And if he's not in the palazzo, he's somewhere else around here." Betty tried the door of the palazzo and the heavy wooden door swung open silently. They stood in the middle of the mosaic-covered floor and listened. The place was silent. "Phyllis! Lester!" Margaret called, and waited, but no one answered.

Betty said, "If Max stabbed Benedict in the back, and pushed his body into the pool, why did he leave the painting and those sketches behind? What's the point of murdering to acquire a valuable object and then not taking it away?"

"Because he planned to return and get it. He might have thought that no one would find the body so quickly, and just wanted to get away from the scene. Anyhow, I believe he has now retrieved the painting."

Just then, they heard voices and soon Phyllis, Lester, and Blum, trailed by Giulia, entered from the frescoed room.

"Miss Trenka! You're all right," Phyllis said, a bit too loudly. "We've been searching the upper floors for you."

"I'm not quite all right," Betty said. "I was drugged and kidnapped and stashed in the chapel. And I'm sorry to say that Benedict Howe was found murdered in a fountain right after he kidnapped me."

Phyllis took a deep breath but didn't otherwise react to the news. "Ben is dead? But what about my portrait?"

Lester did not seem to be much troubled by this development, but Josef Blum was definitely startled.

"How did it happen? How do you know he was murdered? He was helping me with some important business here."

"The theft of the reputed Raphael Madonna, perhaps?" Margaret said.

"Lady Margaret, I am a respected dealer. I do not need to steal. And I am inclined to believe that this painting is not genuine. It has certain characteristics that support its authenticity, but others that . . . make it doubtful."

"I wonder when you had the opportunity to come to this conclusion," Margaret said. "When did you see it?"

"That is no concern of yours," Blum said sharply. Margaret scowled so fiercely, however, that he went on, "As it happens, the delightful Principessa Olympia—" Surely, Margaret thought, there was very little that was delightful about Olympia "—invited me to visit the chapel where the painting was housed.

I arrived here earlier than the Floods. Max and Benedict had already encountered her and introduced me. She graciously consented to show me the picture while Ben did some preliminary sketches that he intended to prepare on authentic paper with authentic media—"

"Forge, you mean," Margaret said, "so you could sell them to gullible collectors as genuine Raphael sketches."

"My dear lady, don't sound so outraged. It's a common enough practice if the artist has the talent. Ben certainly did. There are a number of dealers who would welcome his contributions to art. Of course he was less skilled than Eric Hebborn, who also came to a bad end right here in Rome. Hebborn managed to fool experts around the world with his forgeries for years. I was hoping to bring Ben along to that point."

"Then Ben's career was ended abruptly," Margaret said, "presumably by your friend Max Grey, who now has possession of the doubtful Raphael."

"Max? He and Ben were good friends, had been for years, ever since Max turned up in Rome after his father arranged to have him spirited out of England after that unfortunate business with the children. The English don't like people troubling their little ones, and he also did some damage to a couple of dogs. Cruelty to animals really disturbs the English. Just boyish pranks, but his father thought he would be better off out of the country permanently, in some place where people aren't so fussy. I've known the family for some time. Max actually introduced me to Ben, and we went into a little business together. It's impossible to believe that Max would stab Ben in the back."

The Floods had drawn back the ragged curtain and were gazing out the window at the landscape, so they were not listening to Blum. Phyllis, however, was beginning to show signs of restlessness, and perhaps even a little grief over the death of Benedict. Lester was resolutely refusing to comfort her on the demise of her demiparamour-cum–resident artist. Blum strolled off to join them.

"What do we do now?" Betty asked. "It does seem to me suspicious that Mr. Blum knew that Benedict had been stabbed in the back. We didn't mention it, did we? Could Blum have done it, and if so, why? Ben was a good source of income. He had all that old paper he stole from Priam's Priory. He could have produced a pile of forgeries."

"That damned painting," Margaret said. "Blum wanted to get his hands on it, without having to pay Ben whatever he might demand for stealing it. If he would go to such murderous lengths to get it, he must be convinced that it is genuine. A fake would just cause him trouble if he tried to sell it as the real thing. Some expert would prove it wasn't real."

"Since he and Max don't appear to be very up-right and honest people, especially Max, it could be that if Blum committed the murder, he would concoct a tale to point the finger of guilt at Max. Or maybe they did it together."

"And who bashed the *principessa*?"

"Whoever wasn't busy prying the panel from the frame when the princess decided to defend her possession. I think it's time that we got the authorities involved in this little group," Margaret said firmly.

"I don't suppose that Phyllis and Lester had anything to do with the crime," Betty said.

"Lester said he wanted the picture, but not, in the end, enough to commit murder. People like the Floods take a fancy to something just because they can afford it, but if they're denied, something else will soon look just as good to them. I'm certain, for example, that there are any number of starving artists who would be glad to paint on demand any type of picture they want for Rime Manor. Benedict was just conveniently there for them. And Phyllis was bored with the country and thought a brush with a bohemian lifestyle might be a pleasant diversion. There are other diversions available to her."

CHAPTER 19

*I*T WASN'T necessary to send to the villa for the authorities. A young, heavy-featured man who looked very official accompanied Prince Aldo to the room.

"Mamma is fortunately not seriously hurt," he said. "She has gone to the villa with Giulia to rest. I sent Luca off to the fountain with the medical people to retrieve the body. I wish I knew what had become of the painting. I curse myself for leaving it when the alarm sounded, but at least I was there quickly to comfort Mamma."

Blum heard him speak, and suddenly looked pleased. Betty had a clear picture in her mind of Max slinking through the gardens to the fountain, snatching up the panel with the painting, and making off to the red car, through the village, and back to Rome. It would cost Blum a mountain of lire to get it from him. But why was she standing here thinking about what might have happened?

"Margaret, to the car park, or Max will get away with it."

Arthritis or not, Betty raced out of the palazzo, followed by Margaret, and cut across the parkland down the hill to the car park at the bottom. Prince Aldo and a police person were not far behind. The red sports car was still there. Betty stopped. "I was so sure he'd try to get away with the picture."

"But we don't even know for certain that he has it or where he is," Margaret said.

"Although the painting was gone when I reached the fountain, these were still there." Aldo showed the bundle of sketches that Ben had done.

"Max and the picture must be somewhere around the estate or in the village. Where?" Betty asked.

"The *contadini* will search the few farm buildings. I think, Miss Trenka, that I will disturb Mamma's rest and bring her to the village. The villagers will do anything for her, anything she asks. So if she asks them to give up Max, they will do so if he is hiding there."

"Why didn't he take the car?"

"Perhaps it would be too easy to identify it in Rome. Everybody knows Max's car," Betty said. "Even the prostitutes recognize it."

"But," Margaret said, "he might have chosen to go to Mirella and Piero's home. It's on the way to Rome. No one would think of looking for him there."

"Piero Pannini was desperate to add the painting to his collection," Betty said. "Josef told me so. If Max asked a lower than expected price for it, Piero might have given him sanctuary in exchange for the bargain."

Margaret said, "I am still convinced that Josef Blum killed Ben, aided by Max."

A short time later, Principessa Olympia, having heard an explanation from the prince, emerged from the villa in her dusty black dress leaning on Giulia's arm. She consented to be driven to Ingranno and she, the prince, Margaret, and Betty proceeded to the village with Luca at the wheel. Olympia still shot venomous looks at Betty and Margaret from time to time, even as her son reassured her that the ladies were simply visitors, without a thought of marriage.

"We must get our Madonna back for the chapel," Aldo said, "and you must apologize to Miss Trenka for kidnapping her."

Olympia merely looked out at the passing scenery.

They drove slowly into the village and stopped at an outdoor cafe. The old men sitting at the tables with their cups of espresso and glasses of wine took off their hats out of respect for the princess.

Aldo got out of the car and addressed them in Italian. "An English boy has stolen something valuable from the *principessa*. She asks that you find him if he is hiding in the village and give him up to the police, then return the picture he has stolen to the Castrocanis."

The men nodded, but no one got up to search for Max.

"He passed through Ingranno earlier today," Aldo said, "in a red *macchina*."

Now the men were consulting with each other in low voices.

"We saw him in the red car, but he is not here," one

of the men said. "We want to help the *principessa*, but we cannot. We do not know where he is."

"The bus from Rome arrives in ten minutes, and then leaves again for Rome in another ten minutes," Luca said. "Maybe he will go to Rome on it. In that case, he must be hiding in the village, ready to jump on board while the bus driver drinks an espresso."

"He asked about the vineyards when he passed through," one man said. "He said he had heard that Ingranno had better wine than Frascati."

"He went into Tullio's shop," another said. "Hey, Tullio, what did he buy from you?"

"He bought a knife," a hefty, balding man said. "Him and the other boy who was with him. I told them not to take cuttings from the vines or the olive trees, and they just laughed and said they were cutting something more valuable."

Then the *principessa* spoke and the men leaned forward to listen.

"You will find this *cattivo* and bring him to me bound like a chicken. I will have my revenge, and you know that I will. You know what I am willing to do to my enemies."

"*Si, si, principessa.*" The men talked again among themselves, and then two or three stood and drifted away.

"They will find him, if he is still in the vicinity, and they will get their wives and children to help," Aldo said. "Let us return to the villa. Mamma is tired, and there is nothing more we can do here."

As Luca drove them back up the hill, Margaret said, "It's not possible, is it, that your mother might have had a hand in killing Ben? She seems to have a bloodthirsty reputation."

Olympia opened her mouth and began to rant. Clearly she understood more English than she let on.

"She says you are *brutta* for suggesting such a thing, Margaret. No, I am certain she was lying nearly unconscious in the chapel along with Miss Trenka, who was half-drugged herself when Benedict Howe was murdered. The only possible suspects are Max and Josef Blum. We know where the one is, but not the other."

Betty said suddenly, "He—Max—went to . . . to a safe place. We need to get back to the palazzo quickly if we are to find him."

"What do you mean by a safe place?" Margaret asked.

"Don't you remember what the princess said after she reported that the *ragazzi* disturbed her siesta?"

"I have it," Margaret said excitedly. "She said she told them to 'go to the olive tree, or I will punish you.' You remember, Aldo. You showed us the old olive tree, and told us that you and later Paul used to climb up and hide among the leaves when you misbehaved. Your mother mentioned it as a hiding place, so that's where Max has gone. He must have been lying about near the fountain when we found Ben, and when you left the painting behind, he took it away. He didn't drive away so he's hiding high up in the branches under those silver leaves. Let's hurry before he can get to his car and escape."

"The police are watching the car," Aldo said. "He can't escape that way. The villagers will watch the bus, so that exit is closed to him. Perhaps his only hope is to lie low and hope that Blum will help him. I have heard that they are very intimate friends."

They piled into the car and Luca sped them back up the hill. The grounds around the palazzo were covered with police, but no one was near the old olive tree that didn't belong in the parkland but had been there for five hundred years.

"I want to be the one who captures him," Aldo said. "Not only did he contrive to steal my property and damage my mother, but he is responsible for ruining a very fine new suit."

It was an almost sheepish Max Grey who climbed down carefully from the gnarled old olive tree after it had been surrounded by an army of men—police and Aldo's farm laborers. He had been well hidden, since from a distance there was no way he could be seen, but when Prince Aldo stood at the foot of the tree and looked up through the twisted branches, he saw Max clutching the painting and clinging to a sturdy limb of the tree.

First Max refused to answer the calls for his surrender, but when Josef Blum was summoned to plead with him, he gave up and made his way down. It was to Blum that he handed the picture, not the prince.

"We almost made it, Josef," Max said. "And don't pretend that you weren't at the heart of the scheme, and don't pretend that you didn't urge me to kill Ben. You were willing to give up all the money you could have made from his forgeries for the sake of this single picture." Josef Blum looked taken aback by his treachery. Max continued, "I don't rank as an expert, but I do know a little, and so did Ben. He knew quite a lot, because it was his business to know what was real and what was not.

"Ben looked at the painting closely, and, I'm sorry to disappoint you, Prince Aldo, Ben concluded that this is *not* an original Raphael. In fact, you will find that it is a twentieth-century forgery—produced many centuries after Raphael's death—by someone highly skilled in forging the Master's work. Ben even said he was certain who had forged it. All of this business was pointless. I'm sorry for you, too, Josef. You murdered Ben, when I wouldn't, all for the sake of a fake."

"I didn't kill him. You did." Josef's voice had turned a bit hysterical.

"You did, Mr. Blum," Betty said. "I'm beginning to remember what I heard in the chapel when you all thought I was unconscious. It went something like this. Max said:

" 'Hurry, Ben. Get the panel out of the frame. Then you and I will take it down the hill in back to that big fountain. Josef will bring the car around by the drive that the old lady blew up during the war. We'll lie low until it's dark then bring the picture around to the car and head for Rome. Don't worry about the old ladies. Someone will find them eventually.'

"Then I heard Ben say, 'But now that I have my hands on the picture, I'm not handing it over to Josef, and I'll tell him just that when I see him. It's mine and mine alone. I'll sell it to old Piero for what I can get, or even Flood.' "

Betty smiled as Max scowled at her and said, "That's not exactly what Ben said, but it's generally accurate. He definitely did say that the painting was his, and his alone."

"Then you all were gone," Betty said. "I suppose it was then that Josef argued with Ben about the painting, and Ben died for it. I'd guess we'll find that the knife is the one the boys bought in the village. Eventually, Josef sent Max to pick up the picture and he went to hide in the olive tree until dark, while Josef tried to be so helpful in the searches."

"I wonder," Margaret said, "whether the Raphael was actually forged by Ben himself."

"But the painting was in my family's hands for centuries," Aldo said. "It couldn't be a twentieth-century forgery. How could the original have been replaced by a fake? And if it was, where is the original?"

Margaret said gently, "Maybe it is hanging in a big white house in Dallas. Maybe when Paul was young and a friend of Ben's, he let him into the chapel, and Ben made a copy that he turned into a forgery when he was skillful enough. You said that Carolyn Sue had always wanted it to be a Raphael, Aldo. So she arranged to have it copied and put in the chapel, then took the original away with her when you divorced. Then she was free to have it authenticated. Ben knew the painting in the chapel was a fake without looking at it because it was his own work. He couldn't simply reproduce his own fake because he'd need the right materials and a lot of time to age it. Maybe even Max knew, but Josef didn't, so he murdered Ben to get what he thought might be a genuine Raphael. I'm sorry, Aldo, that you didn't win the lottery after all."

Prince Aldo said, "Thanks to Carolina, I didn't even have a lottery ticket. You ladies must be tired, and I beg your forgiveness for the trouble we put you to. Mr. Blum will have to extricate himself from his difficulties. I'm sure the charges will be many and serious for Blum and for Max."

"I have been told that Blum has important connections to draw on to help him resolve his problems," Betty said. "I don't know that mere connections will resolve a matter of murder."

"Luca, bring the car around and return my guests to Rome," Aldo said. "I was beginning to hope, Margaret, in spite of my mother, that we might become better acquainted. Well, it would not be wise now because of Carolyn Sue and the painting. But I intend to fly to America very soon and confront her about it. I don't think I could convince the authorities that she robbed me, because we were still married at the time, but maybe I can persuade her to return it. Appeal to her good nature and sense of honor and fairness."

"I'm afraid both are in short supply, Aldo," Margaret said. "Maybe if you recruited Paul to assist you. He is not so well supplied with her money as he once was, so he doesn't have as much to lose. He might be willing to help."

"Then I have another and better excuse for a trip to America. I will see you in New York. Maybe I can recruit you to help as well."

Margaret said, "Carolyn Sue is also fond of Betty, so you will have another ally."

The prince kissed Margaret's hand as they entered the car. Betty thought that terribly sweet, but Principessa Olympia almost growled at the sight.

Then they were on their way back to Rome.

"I think I'd like to visit the Pantheon again," Betty said, "to pay tribute at Raphael's grave. And remind him that he should not rest in total peace because of the matter of Prince Aldo's ruined suit."

CHAPTER 20

BY THE time that Betty was home in East Moulton, Connecticut, she had seen enough fine art, baroque churches, Renaissance palaces, and stately statues to last a lifetime.

"The Vatican and Saint Peter's were truly remarkable," she told Ted Kelso. "We went to Saint Peter's Square on a Sunday and even saw the pope on the balcony. I sent Sister Rita several postcards mailed from the Vatican, and she told me she received them very quickly. They say the Vatican postal service is rather more efficient than Rome's. Now where was I?"

Ted said, "Talking about the murder and its resolution. I don't believe you heard all that stuff while you were knocked out in the chapel."

"Oh that," Betty said. "I was sure Josef and not Max had done the murder, so I decided to do what I do best."

"And that is?"

"Be someone I'm not. A fake, a fraud, a forged Betty Trenka. I was supposed to be unconscious, so I simply forged an image of myself as being awake.

214

I did hear a few words, you know. Blum confessed in the end, because he thought I was telling the truth."

"Brave girl," Ted said. "Do you know if Carolyn Sue found out whether the picture she absconded with is a genuine Raphael?"

"Margaret asked her, but she declined to comment. I suppose if it's not genuine, she can still tell people it is. If it is real, she has the satisfaction of knowing she has it and Aldo has a fake. I don't suppose the value means much to her. She must have thought she was very clever by finding young Benedict, her son's friend with a gift for forgery. The painting certainly looked real rather than a fake to me."

"Now let's take a fake walk," Ted said. "I can manage about ten steps, but tomorrow it may be twenty, and then thirty."

"I'm glad to be home," Betty said. "Margaret resisted staying on in Rome for another week or two. Prince Aldo is very charming, and he even brought his mother into the city to treat us to lunch before we left. Aldo said they'd put the forged Raphael Madonna back in the chapel, and his mother doesn't care at all whether it's real or fake. And Margaret swore a solemn oath to her, right on the Via Veneto at a charming sidewalk cafe, that she wouldn't marry Aldo, which pleased Mamma greatly.

"Phyllis and Lester Flood scurried back to England in a great rush, but not before Phyllis found a very handsome young Italian artist who jumped at the chance to become the Floods' resident painter. I don't know what became of Max. He just disappeared into *la dolce vita* again. Perhaps he had better connections than even Blum. He may be lying by a pool in Marrakech with *il marchese* at his side."

"How about that walk?" Ted said, and Betty watched him strain to stand. When he was on his feet, he reached for his metal crutches and walked—actually walked—slowly and carefully to the back door to the garden. "Elizabeth, allow me to show you my garden—that is, if you haven't had your fill of gardens."

"I'd love to, Ted. I feel as though we've both won the lottery."

Did you like *Forged in Blood*?
Then don't miss. . .

A BETTER CLASS OF MURDER
The first mystery starring
Lady Margaret Priam and Betty Trenka

by Joyce Christmas

Lady Margaret Priam and Betty Trenka solve a
high-tech Manhattan murder among the very rich.

Please turn the page. . .

Published by Fawcett Books.
Available wherever books are sold.